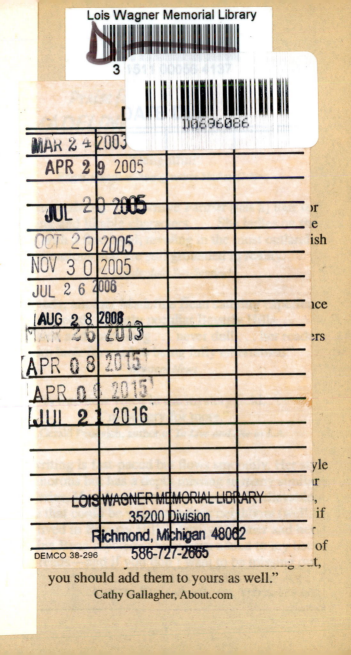

or
e
ish

nce

ers

yle
ur
,
if
r
of

you should add them to yours as well."
Cathy Gallagher, About.com

JERRILYN FARMER

DIM SUM DEAD

**A MADELINE BEAN
CATERING MYSTERY**

AVON BOOKS
An Imprint of HarperCollinsPublishers

To Evelyn Kobritz and William Sarnoff,
my role models—
for Evelyn's beauty and strength
and Bill's jazzy spin on life

ACKNOWLEDGMENTS

There would be no Mad Bean books without my closest advisor, my wonderful husband, Chris. Through some insanely dizzy days, he encouraged me to do more than I have ever before attempted, and then tirelessly cleaned up the wreckage when, on occasion, I hit the wall. The result: cities were visited and signings were held; a successful mystery writing class was taught at UCLA Extension; another fabulous season of *Supermarket Sweep* was written; two healthy, happy boys excelled in grades 1 and 4; and the completion of this book you are now holding. My luckiest day was the day I met my husband. This book is for Chris, with my love and deepest thanks.

I am also happy to acknowledge the contributions of Chef Nick, who learned to read while this book was being written, and to Strategy Advisor Sam, whose deep philosophical conversations kept his mom's brain percolating. This book is also for Sam and Nick, with my love.

I have to thank all my cousins, but particularly Emily Silver and Miriam Becker, for showing me how strong and accomplished the women in our family can be. This book is for Emily and Minky and the Sarnoff/Sornoff cousins, with love.

As always, I must thank my editor, Lyssa Keusch, for her exceptional talent and a friendship I treasure. I must also thank my excellent literary agent, Evan Marshall, whose advice and jokes and gossip and brilliance I cannot do without.

"*I* hate surprises." I do. Hate 'em.

My best friend and partner, Wesley Westcott, had just arrived at the Santa Monica Farmer's Market to meet up and buy supplies. He pulled off his backpack and propped it up next to a dark forest of fresh romaine and a spiky rustle of gray-green endive.

"You always say that," Wes said, "but this one is different."

"I don't think so."

Our breath misted when we spoke. Southern California in January. Who said we don't have seasons? But, of course, the day would warm up. As soon as the sun burned through the fog, we'd make it up to seventy degrees, warmer inland.

I put a crisp Chinese cabbage back down upon a perfect pyramid display of similar heads. "Really, Wes. I hate surprises."

Wes began to unzip the black bag now resting on the outdoor vegetable cart. "Stop saying 'hate.' "

"Okay. I don't want to be negative. Negativity sucks. But . . ."

A small man, examining some chard, looked up. His dark eyes gave me a once-over before they returned to their careful examination of greens.

I lowered my voice. "I just want to point out that surprises are highly overrated. In my opinion."

"You just like to know everything ahead of time. That's

line Bean Events, because, you know, it sounds more digni-
fied. He didn't think dignity "sells" particularly well here in
L.A. Perhaps he's right, because we are doing just fine as
Mad Bean Events, catering Hollywood parties and planning
a kicky range of ultra-high-end special events.

For Wesley and me, the Santa Monica Farmer's Market is
one of our Wednesday morning rituals. It's something we've
done since we moved down to L.A. from Berkeley nine
years ago. We both love food and we both love to shop—so
this was just about heaven for us, if you didn't mind thousands of other shoppers elbowing you aside to get the last
ripe Haas avocado.

The early-morning bustle on Third Street, closed off to
car traffic, was getting thicker by the minute. Tight throngs
of well-dressed Westside gourmets scoured the finest and
freshest fruits and vegetables of the season. One could peo-
ple-watch for hours.

There were the young couples, holding hands, their heads
close together as they whispered about dinners they would
share. There were men, serious home cooks, who shopped in
silence. There were lots of attractive women—young moms
pushing tots, and media career types, and others we like to
call forty-and-holding—everyone carrying designer water
bottles and dressed casually, perhaps on the way to workouts
with their trainers. All over the Market, you'd see them, lifting a melon up for a quick sniff, squeezing a lemon lovingly,
and tucking their dawn buys into the latest lavender Kate
Spade totes.

Shopping along with the neighborhood regulars, of
course, there were a goodly number of us professional chefs,
and we all knew each other. The outdoor Market was a natural place to meet and gossip in the chilly, overcast mornings,
and then to vie like schoolyard bullies for first pick and special buying privileges from our favored grower/vendors.

"Excuse me." A young mom stepped up to the stall and
grabbed a bunch of basil, and resumed talking a kind of
baby talk to the infant she had strapped to her chest in one of
those contraptions. "La-la-la-la-la" this young woman bur-
bled to the infant. I looked closely at the baby. He or she

Wes nodded.

I noticed it was covered with Chinese designs and lettering. "This," I said, studying it, "is very cool."

Wesley leaned the box on a corner of the vegetable stand. He fiddled with the brass lock for a second, then slowly raised the lid. I moved closer.

There, inside the dark case, were stacked dozens of beautiful small white tiles, about three-quarter inch by one and a half inches. They looked like bone or ivory. Hand-etched and colored on the face of each tile was a Chinese character, or a number, or a lovely Asian picture.

"A mah-jongg set." I held out my hand and pulled the brass handle on one of three slender drawers. It slid easily to reveal more of the lovely tile pieces. "And it looks very old."

Wesley smiled.

This happened to be a sweet stroke of serendipity. For the past six months, Wes and I had been catering the very private Sweet and Sour Mah-Jongg Club up in the Hollywood Hills. You may remember mah-jongg if you have any old aunts of the Jewish or Chinese persuasion—in which case, you are now shaking your head. I know. But it turns out the kitsch old game of mah-jongg has become the new hipster obsession. Perhaps it's the hint of the Orient, or the intricate strategy, or the luck, or the gambling. Whatever. Our young clients were hooked.

They had organized a weekly MJ party, which they held at a large estate belonging to a hot young music video director, Buster Dubin, the leader of their pack. They played mah-jongg. Mad Bean Events provided the gourmet grub. It had become one of our smaller but steadier gigs.

I touched the mah-jongg case and picked out one of the tiles. It was exquisitely smooth and cool to the touch. Etched in red on one side was a Chinese pictogram of a sword.

"Wes, this is beautiful."

"The Red Dragon. Yes. I didn't have time to check out the entire set. We just found it an hour ago."

"You were doing demo all night?"

"We've got the plasterer coming in two days. Our schedule is tight. I'll crash on the weekend."

Beneath it, at the bottom of the drawer, was a small book, possibly of mah-jongg instructions, bound in red leather.

"What if it's a jewel box filled with diamonds?" I asked.

Wes tried to loosen the silver lid of the box, but couldn't. He shook it and we heard the muffled clank of metal on metal.

"Does it have a lock?" I asked. A few people in the crowd around us began to take an interest.

There was no lock that either of us could see. I told Wes to hold the small silver box steady, and I edged my thumbnail under the rim of its tightly stuck lid. As he braced the silver case, I pushed up on its lid as hard as I could.

With all that prying force, the lid swung back on its hinge and out flew the contents, landing at our feet. I looked down.

A drop of blood flecked the pavement. And then a few more.

"Maddie, you're hurt!"

"I am?"

I looked at my ankle and noticed the thin red gash, felt the throbbing pain, watched as the drops of blood splashed down on my Nikes. It was true. I had been cut.

A woman a few steps away gasped.

On the pavement lay the object that had fallen from the silver box. It looked very old. It had a long curved blade. It was an antique Chinese dagger with a handle carved in the shape of a dragon.

I hate surprises.

And then something magical happened. My focus abruptly shifted from my ankle to my left hand as something lovely and warm clamped onto me in a tight, hot grasp.

I looked down. A perfectly beautiful, towheaded child of about three was hanging on to me for dear life. The child had simply grabbed on as he looked around the open-air market, his attention fastened to the large Gala apples on the stall beside us. I was astonished. Did children this little really have such strength? Such heat?

Just then, the boy looked up into my eyes. His were a clear and brilliant shade of soft denim blue. I looked down in surprise on his lovely face.

His expression froze. I was not his grown-up. His mother, paying for some purchases a few feet away, must have been the intended target of that tight little hand. He let go of me fast, and the electricity in our connection vanished. I watched him, blond and angelic, as he quickly found his mommy, and she soon felt the warmth of her baby's hand.

Wesley, missing that little scene, was staring at me. "You look weird, Mad. You sure you're okay?"

Was I? I was having a strange moment, that's for sure. But it had nothing to do with the nick to my ankle. So, is that what some women feel about babies? That fierce thrill? I had to wonder.

"Wesley?"

We both turned. The voice belonged to a friend of ours, Jody Silva, a grower with a stand a few steps away.

"You got a minute?" Jody asked. She had come out from behind the stall. She was a young woman who was built on a heavy frame, but a strong one. Her muscles had been developed not on a weight machine but by lifting crates at her family's farm and loading them into her truck. "We've got a lady customer. She bought a case of potatoes for this camp she runs for sick kids. We give her a real good price, but she needs to get the load over to her pickup."

"Would she like a hand?" Wesley asked, looking up and spotting the customer, standing by her crate of potatoes not far away.

"Could you do her this favor?" Jody asked.

etable stand, throwing a hand up at the very last second to prevent the sharp wooden rim from poking out an eye. Under the sudden weight, the leg beneath the table buckled. I heard Jody's voice, now shrill. "Stop that! Get security! Stop him!"

I tried scrambling up to my feet, as the squash and cucumbers toppled down onto me. The sweatshirt man, standing close by, tried to help me up.

"*Maddie!* You okay?" Jody called, her voice full of tension.

Jody's sister started screaming from the other end of the booth. "I told you. It's not safe here. The homeless! They're everywhere in Santa Monica . . ." She continued rattling on more of the same, as her urban paranoia ratcheted up to a dangerous high.

I looked back to the ground to pick up my things.

Hell.

"Wesley's case! *Hey!*" I squinted after the form of a short man walking fast as he disappeared into the thick crowd down the lane. "That guy who was pushing—he took off with my stuff!"

"What?" Jody looked in the right direction but it was too late to see him by then. At the top of her lungs, Jody began yelling, *"THIEF! Thief!"*

People nearby stopped talking. Some helpful souls had been righting the tipped produce stand, arranging to fix it to stand level again. Meanwhile, Jody began blowing a high-pitched whistle. "They'll stop him, Maddie," she said, and shrieked her whistle again.

I didn't stick around to find out if the law of the Santa Monica Farmer's Market would work its magic. I took off after the man, who by now had gotten lost in the crowd.

I picked up some speed, cutting to the center of the road, avoiding the stalls and the main clusters of shoppers. I couldn't see the thief, but there was no place for him to have turned off, yet.

I should have been more careful, more alert. I usually was. I was engulfed by the crowd, now, unable to see two feet in front of me. Damn!

I pulled away from him. More time lost.

I backed up and spun around off the curb, but before I could take off down the road, I was intercepted again. This time, by another man. Only this man was sitting on a bicycle—a young, good-looking man wearing shorts, with the kind of thigh muscles that could make a heart flutter. Not that I notice these things. I was now looking at a sworn officer in the Santa Monica Police Department Third Street Bicycle Patrol. His badge read, "Stubb."

Officer Stubb pulled to a stop beside me. "Your name Maddie?"

"Madeline Bean, how . . . ?"

"They gave a description," Stubb explained.

"What?"

"Your long braid. Your gray jeans. Your great . . ." Stubb stopped the description at the point of embarrassing himself. "One of the vendors reported the theft. We've got our guys out on bikes, but there are a lot of people here at the Market today. We've got to take it slow."

"I just saw the jerk," I said, frustrated as hell. "He went there, off to the left. We've got to move fast."

"We're on it," Stubb said, resisting my command to move fast or even budge. "I've got two officers on that part of the Market. They'll get the guy. It's hard to run through a place like this without attracting attention."

"They've just got to find him," I said, more to myself, and took another quick glance at Stubb.

I knew about the Santa Monica cops on wheels. They were a PR guy's dream: seventeen hunky officers selected for their interpersonal skills and riding ability. They were highly visible—a comfort to any nervous sightseers about to leave their tourist dollars in the beach city that was also known for its homeless "element."

But I was freaking out, just standing around, doing nothing. I looked up and read concern in the nice brown eyes of young Officer Stubb.

"Sorry," I said. "I have got to get that box back to my partner. I'd better go out there and look for it."

"Miss Bean," Stubb explained calmly, "agility, maneuver-

that. Why don't I just go down the street there"—he gestured to the left—"and maybe we'll get lucky."

"Sure."

"So, what is it I'm looking for? The stolen property?"

"Mah-jongg tiles. It's a game. They were in an antique Chinese chest about this big." I made a halfhearted gesture showing him about eighteen inches high and twelve inches around. "It's an old wooden box with brass hooks and latches. My friend left it with me for a minute, and then this bizarre little man shoved me down and grabbed it."

"Okay, then. I'll check it out."

Young, huge Officer Stubb had the decency to look rather pink about the face as he wheeled his bike around in the proper direction. He spoke into his radio once again. Perhaps he was finally calling in some megawheels backup, like a patrol car, to head the guy off. But I wasn't counting on it. After all, I'd only lost a "march on" set. This wasn't grand theft, auto.

But what was I going to tell Wesley?

I trotted down the street, passing vendors and shoppers, looking ahead for any sign of the missing thief, or Wesley's antique mah-jongg set, or Officer Stubb's police buddies. In about a block I reached a dead end and I could only turn left or right. In such cases, I make it a habit of always turning to the right. I jogged down the stalls on the one side, and wove my way through the stalls on the other. Nothing. *Nada.* Zilch.

I should have turned left. Figures. It was just that kind of day. I doubled back and raced over to the next block, feeling the sense that too much time had slipped away and I'd never be able to make this one up to Wesley. I was just too lame. So of course, I kept running. I retraced my steps and did the entire circuit one more time, telling certain vendors I knew to keep a lookout for the box.

And when I found myself at the very end of the Third Street Promenade, all the way south, near the entrance to Santa Monica Place shopping mall, I stopped. I had been running around in circles for fifteen minutes, and running pretty hard.

I leaned over, hands on my knees, and gulped some air.

I stopped inside the entrance and flipped open my cell phone. I had to tell Wesley the bad news sometime.

"Wes here," he said. That's his phone schtick. I liked it, so businessman and cordial.

"Madeline here," I replied. "I'm still in Santa Monica."

"Whazzup?" He said it in that disgusting, guttural slangy way that had become popular in a series of beer commercials. We are annoying in this way. We pick up on every fad and buzzword and insist on torturing each other with them. Yes, we are cruel.

"Whazzup?" I said back, being as obnoxious as he was. "Wes, get ready for a big fat horrible story." I was standing near a large planter in the mall.

"What's up?" he asked, his voice instantly full of concern.

I told him the tale.

"So that's it?" Wes asked when I finished. "Your cute bike cop didn't come through?"

"I wish Stubb hadn't stopped me, Wes. I was this close to grabbing the guy." Okay, slight exaggeration. "And I recognized the son of a bitch."

"You did? What do you mean?"

"That guy fingering the chard—did you notice that guy? At Maria's stand. What was his problem?"

And as I was venting and generally acting cranky, standing just inside the mall entrance with shoppers flowing by in ones and twos, I looked up. And there he was. The son of a bitch. He was walking out of Robinsons-May, holding something bulky in a large navy blue Robinsons-May shopping bag.

"Wesley, Wesley, Wesley," I hissed rapidly into the phone, interrupting whatever he was saying. "It's him." He was only about a hundred feet away, walking deeper into the mall, away from where I stood.

"Call the cops." Wes had that stern sound I rarely hear.

"Call you back," I said, and clicked off.

I followed the chard guy, but it was easy this time. The mall was hardly busy this early in the morning. And, even better, the chard guy wasn't on alert. He hadn't seen me. He didn't think he was being followed. He was acting all normal, walking slowly, trying to fit in.

"*That's . . . my . . . bag.*" I shouted, emphasizing each word. "It's mine. Look in the bag if you don't believe me."

The mother was in a difficult spot. On the one hand, she rightly bitched to her kid that he shouldn't be taking trash out of trash cans. On the other, she couldn't stand to have some stranger take something away from her boy. The life of a parent is terrible 'ard, I say.

But I was bigger than Alex, and I was more determined. "Let *GO*!" I pulled at the bag with force.

"Hey, hey!" The mother was aghast at my rudeness. She suddenly realized I was going to escalate this fight over trash. "Let go of the bag, Alex," she instructed her kid more urgently. What a monster I was. I was willing to steal garbage from a baby. "Let go. This woman is crazy. Let her have all the trash she needs. Remember what I told you about Santa Monica?"

Oh, my word.

"Aw, Mom." But Alex obviously remembered how homeless people dig in the trash. He let go of his prize.

They both glared at me with Republican stares, but I didn't care. I turned my back on them and started to look inside the Robinsons-May bag.

It was there. My box. Wesley's box. The hidden-behind-a-wall box. The stolen box. I had it back at last.

"Aw, Wesley . . ." I knew he was feeling bad.

"I didn't want to leave the case in my parked car," Wes continued. "I figured someone might see it and break into the station wagon. Great thinking."

"You can't blame yourself," I said. "We were out in public in daylight. No one can predict random crime."

"I hadn't expected we'd find a knife inside. So I didn't realize . . ."

Wes felt bad for getting me in trouble, and I felt bad for getting him in trouble.

"I'm sorry I lost your stuff, Wesley." Guilt is a really bad feeling.

"That stuff wasn't even mine, really," Wes said. "I was planning to give it back to the home's previous owner."

We'd been talking about this most of the day.

"Maybe we should put this aside for a minute and get back to work," I suggested.

"Right. You're right."

Wes resumed measuring ingredients for the Chinese Turnip Cakes we were preparing. Tonight, being the first night of the Chinese New Year, seemed to demand we create something extra-special for the mah-jongg club.

We were gathered, as we so often are, in the kitchen of my old Spanish house in Whitley Heights. I live in a historic area that straddles the Hollywood Freeway near the Cahuenga off-ramp. In the twenties and thirties, celebrities and film people built Mediterranean mansions and modest Craftsman-style bungalows side by side over the low brown-green foothills. These days, it's still a cool neighborhood, home to an eclectic mix of dog lovers and gay couples and studio folk, from art directors to musicians to that woman who does all the cartoon voice-over work.

Unfortunately, in the past fifty years, downtown Hollywood has taken a nosedive in class. The streets below Whitley Heights have become funky and colorful. Someone more sensitive to grime might even describe them as dirty and dangerous. But I like to think of the transitional nature of these streets as a blessing in disguise. To those of us who couldn't afford to buy a house in any other upscale section

doubt we'll ever see that old Dragon dagger again. Or the silver case. I'm so sorry, Wesley."

"Please, Mad. I told you. It was my fault."

Wes and I had spent most of the afternoon at the Santa Monica police station giving descriptions of what we could recollect. In the end, we were told to go home. They would keep the box, probably just overnight, and dust it for prints. They'd get in touch if they needed more information. One of the department's clerical people looked at my ankle. She had a first-aid box and gave me some disinfectant cream and a Band-Aid. And that was that.

As Wes and Holly kept reminding me over and over since we came home, muggings happen every day. I know that. It's just shocking, that's all. It's shocking when crime brushes against you, even petty crime. But we had a party to prepare for this evening. I had to readjust my focus. And so, we got back to work.

As befitted the Chinese New Year's holiday, our host requested a special feast. Buster Dubin asked us to prepare dinner for twenty. He expected to have four games of mah-jongg going at once, and was ready to set up a fifth if necessary.

"Holly, I think that's plenty of rice flour," I said.

She looked up from her work and said, "Cool." And then she sat down on a tall stool nearby. "So tell me all about this Chinese New Year's thing."

I deferred to Wesley, a man with too many advanced degrees and the kind of memory for detail that can be infuriating when he's remembering *to the word* what you said to him nine years ago, but in all other regards is quite a lovely resource. While Wes explained Chinese New Year, I turned on the computer at my corner desk and found the website I was looking for.

"Chinese New Year is like a combination of Easter and Thanksgiving," Wes said.

"Except, without the turkey, Pilgrims, or cross," Holly guessed.

"True. But food has high significance. Everything that is eaten during this two-week Chinese holiday holds auspicious meaning. Imagine that everything you eat or drink in

or homemade . . . ' " She looked up. "Do we have to make some *lop yok* now?"

"I stopped in Chinatown. Look in the fridge."

"For?" Holly asked.

"*Lop yok* is Chinese bacon."

"Excellent." She brought over the raw bacon, along with a large glass pie pan that we needed to steam it before slicing.

"And the main ingredient?" Wes asked.

Holly scooted over to the list and read: "A two-pound law book." She grinned at him.

"That's *law bok*," Wesley corrected promptly. "Chinese turnip."

Sometimes, whilst cooking, I do believe Wesley may on occasion lose his sense of humor. Holly and I shouldn't tease him, but it's so damn tempting to get a rise out of the guy.

"Not a law book? You're sure?" Holly looked at him.

"Turnip cake," he continued, "is made with Chinese turnip which is called *law bok*. It's a type of *daikon* radish. There is also a *daikon* radish called Japanese *daikon* radish, which is similar to the Chinese turnip in appearance." Wes snickered to himself. "Actually, to make matters even more confusing . . ."

"Could they be?" Holly whispered to me.

". . . translated into English, *law bok* means turnip. Some produce vendors do not realize there is a distinction."

I could imagine the illuminating lectures to which Wesley Westcott must treat such poorly informed vendors and smiled.

"Is it this ugly thing?" Holly asked. She held up a mottled whitish root, about ten inches long and four inches around.

"Right, Holly. The Chinese turnip is more blemished-looking than the Japanese *daikon*."

Holly looked at the root, perhaps to memorize it.

I turned my attention back to the *lop yok*, quickly cutting the raw slab of bacon into thirds. Some people remove only the rind of the Chinese bacon, leaving all the fat. But I find this too rich. I discard the layer of fat under the rind as well. Steaming for about twenty minutes makes it soft enough to dice finely.

and cooking and friends, I couldn't shake the disturbing events of the morning. Surely, on the dawning of the Chinese New Year, this mugging must have some deeper meaning. And, as we finished preparing the Chinese Turnip Cakes, I hoped the signs for our own good fortune might be more auspicious.

"Did you ever get a call back from the police?" I asked Wesley.

He shook his head.

I thought it over one more time. The chard guy got rid of the mah-jongg game as soon as he could, but the dagger and the silver box were missing.

I felt really bad, and I couldn't tell what was making me feel worse—the idea that I had allowed myself to be ripped off in broad daylight at my favorite outdoor market, or the thought that another punk in this big, bad city had his hands on another weapon.

I might mention I almost never see hookers when I drive by, which I find vaguely disappointing from a purely sight-seeing perspective.

In only a couple of miles, however, the street turned trendy. There's a sudden pop-culture rush of giant billboards featuring three-story-high movie posters, or building-sized faces of rock stars. Wes calls this stretch of Sunset "bright lights/big egos." Only when you see a sixty-foot-high painting of Puff Daddy's nose on top of Tower Records do you really know Sunset has fully morphed into the Strip.

To the right of us as we drove slowly west, the Hollywood Hills rose in lumpy prominence. Their winding roads and exclusive neighborhoods were filled with celebrity neighbors. Having survived our bumper-to-bumper drive up Sunset, Wes turned his Mercedes wagon up Doheny. We left the city below for a quick jaunt into the hills.

I looked out my window. Large homes were crammed right next to larger homes on either side of Doheny Drive. Many of the hillside communities placed a premium on land. In this neighborhood, you could buy a house that needed work for a million, and—if you fixed it up—sell it again for a million-three, or a million-five. Lots of upside potential here, the real estate brokers liked to say. I couldn't wait to see Wesley's fixer.

Wes turned onto Wetherbee, one of the narrow side streets that wound up to the right.

"It's a mess," he said. "We're doing everything—new electrical, new plumbing, new roof, new kitchen. We've been ripping the hell out of it. We just pulled out all the cabinets—these sad yellow plywood things put in in the fifties."

"Demolition is fun," I said.

Wesley loved houses. He hated to see a bizarre den addition or bathroom remodel from the dreaded sixties or seventies make a fool of a beautiful old home. It hurt him to discover some lovely early twentieth century architectural gem that had been anachronized over the years by owners who had "modernized."

Wes pulled his car into the driveway of a large Tudor-style house. Against the darkening sky, I could make out the metal

through her that Wesley first learned the Wetherbee house was coming on the market. But, in truth, we didn't know her well. We had never really wanted to.

"She's had a rough year," Wes said.

When Dickey McBride dropped dead from a heart attack last year, their old home had to be sold. Quita mentioned the news at one of the mah-jongg parties. That's how things get done here. Word of mouth. Naturally, Wesley became interested in the property as soon as she described what a wreck it was. And thanks to knowing Quita, he was able to make an offer on it well before it had a chance to make the *LA Times'* Hot Properties column.

"She's kind of a space cadet, isn't she?" I looked at Wes. He had gotten to know her better. They'd had a few conversations as the house moved through escrow.

"She seems spacey. I don't know if that's an act, though. She seems to take care of herself." Wes pulled out his key ring and opened the front door.

Inside, the house was gloomy and darkish. "Sorry. The lights don't work right now. We're in the middle of rewiring."

I walked through the empty entry hall and into the dusty living room. "Oh, Wesley! This place is wonderful."

"Do you like it?" Wes lit a candle and set it down on the mantel of a large fireplace in the living room. "It's got such good bones, don't you think? Look at the ceiling."

Large wooden beams crossed high above. "It must be two stories high."

"Sixteen feet. And we've been able to save the original finish on the beams."

"I love it." I gave my good friend a hug. "You have so much energy. You are amazing."

He folded his arms against the slight chill in the empty room and grinned.

Just then, there was a tap at the door. It had been so light I wasn't sure at first if I had heard anything at all.

"That's probably Quita." Wesley crossed to the entry hall and opened the front door.

In stepped a thin woman. She was "built," as they used to

gretted never having children. With no other heirs, Quita was inheriting the lot. As she was forty-five years younger, it might even be argued that Quita was the "child" Dickey had dreamed of, but let's not go there.

"So your life is moving on," I said cleverly.

"Yes." Quita shifted her off-center gaze from somewhere in the vicinity of Wesley to make eye contact with me, almost. I noticed Quita had watery gray eyes. She was pretty, but something was slightly off, like her tiny kittenlike nose was just a smidge too tiny.

"I would have loved to have seen the house before everything was removed. Wes said it was filled with art."

"I have pictures. Somewhere. In one of my boxes. If you'd like to see them . . ."

"How cool."

I threw Wes a look. I really doubted I'd be spending much time with Quita McBride, going through old boxes and memories. But it was a magnificently odd thought. And Wesley and I love odd.

"I'd like to see any old pictures you have of the place," Wes said. He was the consummate rehabber, always digging for historical references. He pulled out a business card for Mad Bean Events and handed it to Quita. "If you should find any pictures, please give us a call at the work number."

"Have you got anything at all to drink here?" Quita asked.

"Sorry," Wes said. "No. We don't have power right now. And the kitchen's been gutted."

"Oh, of course. That's right. Can I take a look?"

"At the kitchen? Sure. I was just going to give Madeline the tour." Wesley picked up a candle and handed it to Quita. "Just watch your step and follow . . ."

Wes was going to say, "Follow me."

I caught his eye. Damned awkward, if you ask me, leading a widow around her own house especially after one has just finished ripping the place up.

"This must be so horrible for you," I said to Quita, following her down the hallway. I noticed she was almost as tall as Holly is. Man, why is it that I am always surrounded by tall

"I'm sorry about your loss," I said to her. See. I could be nice. "Your husband died only a short time ago, I know."

"Eleven months ago." Quita looked at me and gave me a shy smile. "It was such a shock. So out of the blue. He was healthy. He was very healthy. And then, one night, he was . . . gone."

"So sad," I murmured. I had heard McBride had died in bed. With Quita. That had to be a shock. "How old was he?"

Quita glared at me, suddenly angry. "Yes. I know. He was seventy-five. Everyone talks about that."

Wesley gave me a look which I took to mean "shut up already," but I think people are too afraid of talking about feelings. Of course, Wes has on occasion suggested I am not afraid *enough* of these sorts of conversations, but so be it!

"I read about it in the papers. They said it was his heart."

"Yes, yes, his heart!" Quita tossed off the words. "And, yes, Dickey had a heart condition. I know. You are thinking that I don't want to face reality, and you know what? You are probably right."

I smiled at Wesley. Good therapy was going on here, in this darkened, demolished kitchen.

And then Quita burst out into loud sobs. She clutched at her leaking face with both overly tanned hands, but tears gushed out all the same.

"Oh dear."

I looked at Wesley, who really had the most smug, I-told-you-so sort of grimace on his normally handsome face. "Wes, don't you have any Kleenex?"

Okay, sometimes "good therapy" is wet.

star in Hollywood. Who could blame you for wanting it? Not me. And I guess you can do whatever you want with it. If ripping it up and redoing it is your thing, well go for it. You know? I just miss it. I miss my life. But that's the past. And now that I see it with my own eyes, I think I'm starting to believe it's really all gone. So, anyway . . ."

"Shall we leave the kitchen?" Wes asked.

He led the way back to the front of the house at a sprightly pace. That guy does not like a scene.

Quita's voice had settled down, and her tears had stopped pouring out. "I'll see you both at the party in a little while, right?" she asked us, remembering who we were and what she'd be doing later. "At Buster's house? Oh, I look disgusting. I've got to go change."

"There's time," I said. "Don't worry."

She turned to Wes. "But before I go. Where's my mahjongg case?"

Uh-oh. We knew this was coming. See, Wes had found the antique MJ set upstairs in this house, in the wall of Quita and Dickey's old bedroom. This morning, just before he met me at the Farmer's Market, he had called Quita McBride to tell her the news of his astonishing find. Wes intended to give Quita the stuff he found. He didn't have to, legally. But of course he had wanted to. And now . . . Well . . .

"Quita, I wanted to tell you this in person."

"What?"

"It's about that old mah-jongg set."

"Yes. Dickey's old Chinese antique. I remember it. It was the one we played on when we were first dating." Quita sighed a pretty sigh. "Dickey taught me how to play MJ. I'm so, so grateful you found it for me. I'd been looking everywhere for it. Actually, it's been missing for years."

"Really?"

"That's why I was so annoyed at the Sotheby's people. They're doing the auction for us. The movers brought everything to Sotheby's, and I was sure Dickey's maj set would turn up in the mix. I specifically called and asked them if it was there. They haven't done a complete inventory, and they said I'd have to wait. But now, you found the old maj set!

roo Planet. Big Daddy Roo. And then, that long-ago little girl Quita falling for an old guy who looked, in that film, more marsupial than man.

People are odd, I reminded myself for the trillionth time since I moved to L.A. But this scene was taking odd to a totally new level. An all-time oddness high. I looked over at Wesley who must have been thinking the same thing.

Quita was hard to fathom. She currently had a cute new boyfriend—Buster Dubin, a guy we knew and liked. A young guy with plenty of money and talent. And yet, she still missed the old guy. Maybe love is blind. Or maybe there are some women for whom the best aphrodisiac is fame.

Dickey McBride. I suddenly recalled the bit in *Kangaroo Planet* where Dickey led them all in jet-powered hopping. Sometimes, practiced as I am in the art of restraint in the face of utter absurdity—after all, that is how I make my living—even I cannot keep a straight face. Wes, kindly, avoided making eye contact.

Quita looked out toward the purple and pink impatiens flower border that rimmed the sloped, grassy front lawn. She must have stood in this entry a thousand different times over the past decade, saying good-bye. Only on those other occasions, she hadn't been the one expected to leave.

"But now, about Dickey's MJ set," Quita said, bringing us to the unavoidable subject.

Neither Wes nor I said anything.

I took another tack. "I had no idea that Richard McBride played mah-jongg. How amazing," I said.

"My husband had played mah-jongg for years and years. Literally, from before we were born. He played with some of his dear old friends. You know Catherine Hill?"

Everyone knew Catherine Hill. She was a child star at MGM along with Dickey when he was a young singing, dancing teen heartthrob. She played plucky orphans and poor cousins to Dickey's rich-boy parts in a long series of forties box office hits.

"Your husband played *mah-jongg* with Catherine Hill?" I was astonished.

"She was one of Dickey's regular mah-jongg buddies."

"I think it was a red book." I looked at Wes again.

"Dickey McBride wrote a novel?" Wes asked Quita. "I don't remember hearing about that."

"No, of course you wouldn't have. It was never published. That's the great tragedy. I urged him to write it. We talked about it, you see. Dickey McBride had many talents. He could have been a very great voice in literary fiction. I guess you might say I was his muse. Dickey and I worked on it together—well, I gave him a lot of encouragement. It was a love story. So it had certain meaning to me, you understand? But I never got to read the finished work."

"I see," Wesley said, looking suddenly glummer.

She took a deep breath and went on. "He worked on it for months, scribbling in longhand. He kept the project in a red leather-bound book I gave him as a gift that Christmas. When he finished, he didn't want me to look at it. I begged him to send it to his friend, Daniel Carter, who was the biggest literary agent in the country. It would have been enormous. Dickey McBride's first novel. But, unfortunately, Dickey had a true artist's temperament. Even though his prose was perfect, he himself wasn't pleased with it at all. Not the least little bit. He ended up telling me it was a big mistake. But I know that isn't true.

"He told me he was going to lock the book in his favorite old mah-jongg chest and put it away. I was terribly disappointed. But Dickey did what he wanted to do. I looked and looked for that old mah-jongg set and couldn't imagine where it had gotten to. Now, I realize my darling Dickey had it sealed up in the wall when we were remodeling. That was two years ago. And now, thank God, you have found it at last. May I have it?"

"Well, there is just one small problem."

"What problem?"

"We don't actually have the set Wes called you about. Not right here."

"What is this? Are you two shaking me down or something?" Quita's vague gray eyes glistened with a certain sharpness.

"Of course not!" Wes was shocked.

Chapter 6

Quita stood outside her old mansion on Wetherbee and began breathing irregularly, hyperventilating.

"This man . . ." she said, between trying to slow down her breaths, ". . . who stole the case and the book . . . he . . ." She tried again. "Who was he?"

The chard guy. I knew there was a problem with the chard guy.

"That's the trouble," I said. "He ran off. The police have the mah-jongg case, now, and they're going to do a fingerprint test."

"Oh my God! Oh my God!" Quita had gone extremely white beneath her deep tan. "Tell me this isn't happening. What did he look like?"

"A smallish man, dark complexion. Late forties, early fifties maybe."

And then, right on the front step, Quita sat down hard, buckling into a heap, her purple dress hiking up, revealing long shapely legs.

"What's wrong? What's the matter?" I sat down next to the woman, trying to see if this was one of those situations that required an ambulance.

"Please . . ." Quita gulped. "Please, help me . . ."

Wesley had run down the lawn to his car and fetched back a bottle of Deja Blue water. He untwisted the cap and held it out to the stricken woman seated on the pavement.

"*Who* is?" I asked, stumped. "Catherine Hill?" That legendary old queen bee was seventy at least.

Quita's unfocused gray eyes swept the street, as if there could be some long-retired leading lady out there gunning for her or something. She was sticking with this story. But it didn't make any sense.

"Hey, I'm in trouble here, okay? You don't realize what kind of trouble. I need help. Get that? Either Catherine Hill or one of the other crazy ladies that Dickey used to play mah-jongg with. They hate me. They'd like to see me dead. They think I purposely lured Dickey to have, you know, relations with me that night, even though I knew about his heart condition."

Ah. This was interesting.

"But it's all a load of crap. Look, I have to get away. I won't be safe at Buster's house now." She looked at Wes, her eyes pleading. "Hey, how about this? Let me stay right here at the house. Please. It's perfect. You aren't living here. Everyone knows the house was sold, and I moved out months ago. No one will think to look for me here." She sounded frantic.

I looked at her. Who exactly was Quita McBride really? I had not a clue. It's just a reminder that you never know. You never know who any casual acquaintance really is, do you? Those people who appear on the outskirts of your life, they're a mystery. They seem like anyone else—like your basic regular human. Well, in Quita's case, like your basic regular bored Hollywood wife mah-jongg fanatic type of human. But that's on the outside. On the inside they could very well be a neurotic mixed-up mess, bordering on delusional, and involved in any sort of bad business. It's shocking, though, when you see that other side.

Wesley had a wary look in his eyes. But he used that special, soft voice of his that was so soothing, where he speaks slowly in those low tones. It comes in handy on our party circuit when he must talk some poor overwrought hostess down off of some figurative ledge. I like to think of him as the crazed-female whisperer. He said, "Look around here now. This isn't a house. It's a construction site. Of course you can't stay here. It's not even safe."

need your help? Even though I explained how I can't stay at
Buster's house tonight."

Honestly. How do I get into these things?

"Can't you check in to a hotel?" Wes asked, the voice of
reason.

"They'll trace me from my credit cards. I can't do that! I
know how they trace people." She looked pretty scared.

"Well, here." I slipped my wallet from the back pocket of
my jeans and pulled out several twenties. "Take this."

"What?"

"Go ahead. Check into a hotel somewhere. Don't stay at
Buster's after the party tonight if you're worried about it. Tomorrow morning, you'll feel much better."

Quita looked at the money. "Okay. That's it. I'll slip out
after the party."

"Right. Tomorrow morning, things won't look so bad.
And you can always think it over. Maybe, later, if you are
still worried, you can go talk to Buster."

"No!"

"Or the police."

Wesley looked at me. He thinks I'm soft, always helping
everyone I meet. But even the nutty ones need help. Maybe
especially.

And I started thinking about fate, as I so often do lately.
I've always rejected that notion. I've made fun of my
friends, like Holly, who think we are fated to do this or that.
I believe in self-determination. But maybe we're meant to be
here doing what we're doing. And, so, maybe, if Quita
McBride was meant to be here, having some kind of break-
down, maybe I was meant to be here, too, helping out a
woman who's had a whole lot of bad news lately. But, you
know, at a distance.

"Thanks, Madeline. Thank you."

"And we'll see you at the party tonight. So if you want to
talk some more . . ."

Quita gave us a smile that was almost convincing, then
turned and retreated down the walkway to the curb. She
climbed into a two-year-old yellow Cadillac and pulled
away into the night.

Wes, my oldest and kindest friend, put his arm around me. "I'm not trying to criticize, Mad. I just would love to see you be happy. You spend so much of yourself taking care of others."

"I like others," I said. I do.

"Yes. But you could be a little more particular about exactly which 'others' you allow to get close, eh?"

"I did pretty well when I found you, partner."

"Ah, that you did. And one lucky stroke of genius does not mean you shouldn't be a little more careful now."

Careful? Of course. But I'd heard too many curious things, my brain was itching, and I knew I'd never get to sleep again until I figured out what was spooking Quita McBride.

to be ready by eight. Ray Jackson came down the front steps and met us at the tailgate of Wes's white station wagon.

"I think that's it." Ray leaned against the wrought-iron gate. He was decked out in the same "uniform" all my serving staff wore for informal parties—black pants and white shirts. I believe in self-expression, so there was a fair amount of leeway at casual parties. In Ray's case, he wore black Adidas wind pants and reflective Nikes. His spotless white sleeveless knit shirt exposed dark skin stretched over hard muscles. Ray's shaved head and wide smile made him look more like a well-paid athlete than the just-scraping-by brilliant kid from South Central L.A. that he was. Ray worked many of my parties, earning extra money to help toward a UCLA undergrad degree.

"Are all the tables set up in the Chinatown room?" I asked.

"Yep. Four tables, sixteen chairs, and the buffet and the bar," Ray said. "Hey, check you out, Holly. You're looking fine."

Holly also took liberties interpreting the standard server getup. Her white T-shirt was a tiny thing. With it, she wore low-slung black-linen pajama pants. On her feet were black patent thongs with tiny heels.

Once we were inside Buster Dubin's house, Ray went on to the party room to get things started there. Wes and Holly and I stopped for a minute to talk over who would do what. A fat Buddha sat in the entry, grinning. Even he seemed to sense it was MJ night.

In his exotic decorating style, Buster Dubin didn't just try for a *taste* of the Orient; he indulged in a whole glorious ten-course banquet. Antique bamboo screens sat behind low, black-lacquer tables. An impressive collection of Celedon pottery sat atop ebony chests. Fabulous old silk panels hung on the walls, cream-colored backgrounds featuring scenes of rice fields and cranes taking flight. One wouldn't expect this spare, sophisticated Asian décor to work with the Art Deco Spanish architecture of Dubin's home, but the rich subdued palate of black and cream with accents of pale green was a success. The bro' was not only chillin', as Ray called it, but he had exquisite taste.

How could a guy in his twenties afford authentic antique Chinese art? you may wonder. This is Hollywood, don't for-

"Ladies! Alone at last."

Holly and I laughed.

"Anyone thirsty?" he asked. "Quita has been experiment-ing. She's prepared the Singapore Sling." He gestured to his own pink drink. "I've started to party before my guests ar-rive. I hope you're not shocked."

"Nothing shocks Maddie," Holly replied.

I don't know if I can actually claim that. But I do have a tendency to bounce back rather quickly. Which is a talent, I submit, in our worrisome world. The last couple of days were a perfect example. Look at this morning. Mugged by that chard guy. And look at the odd little scene at Wesley's house with spooky Quita McBride and her tears and her fears. If we were scoring stress points, you might say I have been through rather a lot. And the night was still young, my friends. We hadn't even begun the party yet. So, therefore, I'd have to say finding a host with a drink in his hand preparty was about the least shocking thing I'd seen all day.

"Don't worry," I said to my client. I said these same exact words in this same soothing way thousands of times. It worked like a charm.

Buster visibly brightened. If that was possible.

I said, "We'll have to take a rain check on one of Quita's drinks, though." And I shot a look around. Where was she, anyway?

"Pity. But, then," he whispered, "you probably make one that is infinitely better. Am I right?"

"You may be the judge," I said. "So save some room."

"Tonight's party will be amazing," Holly said. "Did you check your e-mail? Maddie sent out virtual fortune cookies."

"Did you?" Buster looked up from a big gulp of Singapore Sling and smiled, delighted. "Fantastic. I'm going to go up-stairs and log on." He looked at his watch. "Guests will be here in half an hour. So, are you guys okay? Is everything set?"

"Oh, it should be terrific," I said. Caterers must be up. "We're having special and most significant Dim Sum. We have the steam cart and Holly will do the honors."

"Excellent." Buster took a closer look at Holly and his gaze drifted south, seeming to focus somewhere near her ex-posed navel. "Excellent!"

kick back, play a little MJ, win a few bucks . . . you know? Just have a few smiles." He slipped his arm around Holly's bare midriff, which made me frown just a little.

I knew Quita was here, somewhere, and I don't generally like my staff to appear to be upstaging the party host's girl-friend. It is by just such judicious staff management that I have devised to keep on top of the L.A. catering heap. Angry girlfriends/ wives/lovers do not make for repeat business. And some people think the quality of the gourmet cooking is the most important ingredient to catering success. Ha!

"Holly, can you help me in the kitchen?" I picked up my toolbox, filled with my personal collection of cooking im-plements and gadgets and accoutrements.

"Right-o." Holly slipped from the light grasp of our host.

Just then, in a swish of taffeta, descending down the sweeping staircase came Quita McBride. How long she'd been standing at the top landing, I couldn't say.

"Party time?" Quita asked, swishing pink-tinted liquor in her crystal glass, pale eyes dancing from me to Buster to Holly.

Well, wasn't this interesting? Just a couple of hours ago, Quita McBride had told a heartbreaking story of her won-derful memories of old Dickey at the Wetherbee house, but she was now clearly marking her territory around her man.

For his part, Buster easily seemed to share his huge home with a parade of beautiful women. They moved in, they moved out. Quita had only been on the scene a few months. Perhaps she had a more permanent arrangement in mind. What is it about men that the more interesting they are the more messed up their private lives seemed to be? Ah, well.

In the looks department, Quita was quite a startling con-trast to Buster, with her light hair worn long compared to Buster's short shock of blue-black hair. And she was tanned a bit past the point of the current fashion in our health-conscious city, while Buster was quite fair. As for her long body, which was wrapped in a cream-colored slip dress, it was a knockout. Other than her overample chest, the rest of Quita was so wispy thin, she didn't look entirely of this world, while Buster was powerfully built, although perhaps an inch shorter than Quita. They made an attractive couple.

Chapter 8

*B*uster Dubin's kitchen was cramped and old-fashioned, reflecting the lifestyle of a bachelor with little use for anything save a refrigerator to hold take-out leftovers and a microwave to reheat them. It was odd to still be able to find such an impressive older home with such a small kitchen. Remodels usually did away with the original narrow sculleries, which had been suitable enough, at the time they were built, for the help. In current times, these homes fall somewhere north of the two-million-dollar range. For those price tags, most had their old walls bumped out and new cooking palaces installed. But this room's only beauty was the amazing artwork on the new floor.

Wes showed up in the kitchen as Holly and I unpacked the last of our ingredients for tonight's Dim Sum delights.

"Did you hear?" Holly asked him.

"Trouble in paradise," Wes said. "It was hard to miss."

"Did you hear what it was about?"

Wes shook his head. "Something about money. I didn't hear his voice at all. Just hers."

I shook my head. "Exit Ms. Quita McBride. But I do hope they won't go breaking up right now before all the guests arrive. I'm not sure what she would do. Her emotion-o-meter is pegged pretty much all the time."

"Remember, she said she couldn't stay here tonight, after the party?" Wes asked.

We talked that over a bit. It had happened before, the

vited, tantalized, enticed, intrigued, seduced, and flat-out propositioned before being brazenly indulged. Delectable aromas from the kitchen must waft through the house, greeting each guest's sensitive nose. The soft seductive sounds of cutlery on porcelain should underscore the interweaving melodies of happy conversation, all of which provide accompaniment to the host's favored musical background. Dishes must harmonize to provide a wide variety of textures and temperatures, flavors and ingredients. And, the eye's delight upon first spying a dish must be equal to the mouth's delight at how the thing actually tastes. Presentation is key.

Even for a relatively mainstream little item like our Chinese Chicken Salad, we enjoy giving it a unique visual twist. For this particular salad, we do a parody of Chinese take-out. I have white take-out cartons made up that are four times the size of a normal one.

Holly took one of these Giganto cartons out of our supply sack and tipped it on its side onto one of our large lacquer platters. The contrast of the white-cardboard box on the shiny black platter was lovely. Buster would get a kick out of it. The whole oversize scale was fun, and I suspected the idea of gourmet caterers creating fresh culinary delights and then putting them into a take-out container would strike our host as appropriately droll. The salad, when it was completely compiled, would be displayed in the tipped-over carton, spilling bountifully out onto the platter in a lovely large mound. To finish, we'd stick a pair of oversize gold chopsticks into the carton and sprinkle the salad with freshly fried wonton strips.

I watched Holly work, but my mind kept wandering. I usually consider myself a great judge of people. But Quita McBride had had me worried about several things. What was up with her? She had acted so strangely when we told her about the theft of the mah-jongg set back at the other house that she had me spooked.

I know a guy, a detective with the LAPD, and I gave him a call. I had to leave a message. I told him I hoped he might swing by and check out Quita McBride.

picked up what was left of Quita's colorful concoction and poured it down the drain.

Wes was our resident mixologist. "Probably no mixed drink has been as mistreated as the Sling. The only thing most bartenders know about the Singapore Sling is that it's supposed to be pink."

"Ah." Holly looked on as he rearranged the liquor bottles on the table.

"Singapore Sling," Ray said, smiling. "Pleasing groins."

"What?" Wes said, looking up.

Holly gave Ray a wicked grin. "Interesting fantasy life."

"It's an anagram. *Pleasing groins* is an anagram for *Singapore Sling*. Really." He was all teeth. "Betcha didn't know that, Holly."

She was staring at him. "An anagram, huh? How'd you know that?"

"It's just something my brain does naturally. I got the gift."

"You've got the anagram gift." Holly looked from Ray back to me. "Is he messing with me, Maddie?"

I began to laugh. "I always knew Ray was special."

"Thanks, Madeline." He winked at me and turned back to Holly. "*Pleasing groins,* see? Now you'll have something to chitchat about with the guests tonight while we're serving these fancy drinks."

She burst out laughing.

"As I was saying . . ." Wesley waited for his students to settle down, then continued. "The drink was created in 1915 by a Hainanese-Chinese bartender named Mr. Ngiam Tong Boon. Originally, the Singapore Sling was designed to be a woman's drink, hence the attractive pink color. Tonight we'll prepare an adaptation of the original recipe from Raffles Hotel in Singapore."

"That sounds authentic," Holly said, pushing back her bracelets.

"It is. Now look. It's perfectly simple."

We all looked.

Wesley had set up a line of bottles, garnishes, juices, fruit, barware, and ice. "First fill a shaker with ice."

"Ah." Wes put down his glass, satisfied with his work. "A taste of the exotic East."

"Ah!" Holly took another gulp, pleased with herself and enjoying the taste of her first authentic Sling.

"Ah . . . shit!" Ray put his glass down with a grimace. "Man, that stuff is nasty. I mean, that stuff is sweet. And it's . . . pink."

You had to laugh.

Ray caught my eye and shook his handsome bald head. "I suggest that this right here is the prime reason why the nation of Singapore will never be a world superpower."

"Wussy drinks?" I asked, giving Ray's cocktail-political thesis some thought.

"Well?" he asked. "Am I wrong?"

We all told him, "no."

With his head for world politics and anagrams, Ray was sure to go far.

"I'll stick with beer, Wesley," Ray said.

"Well, there's simplicity in that," Wes agreed. "And for those at the party who share your simple tastes, there's a case of Tsingtao on ice."

"Hey, I'd better get to squeezing up some couple dozen limes or I'm gonna be killing myself come show time," Ray said.

Wes and Ray discussed where to set up the bar in the party room and they huddled together packing the liquor bottles and accessories back into the cartons. Ray easily lifted two cartons at once. And then Wes turned to me.

"Madeline. I was just thinking, do we have enough cash to pay the staff?"

Ray, who was almost at the door, stopped. "No problem," he said. "We took care of it."

Holly said, "Maddie always has enough cash to cover the payroll. That's why she's the queen."

It was true, I usually had that stuff wired. Earlier that day I had sent Ray to the bank to pick up the cash we'd need for the party. He brought back a stack of twenties. In fact, I had to talk to him for defacing the bills. He had drawn a tiny frowny face in the corner of each twenty. I showed him my

"Is that Arlo?" Holly asked, looking over at me, mouthing the words.

I nodded.

She pantomimed cutting her throat.

Lucky for me, my friends never try to meddle in my personal life.

"So what do you say we get together later?" he asked.

"I say I've had a rough day."

"Great. Then you'll need a chance to unwind," Arlo steamrollered on.

I added one more item to my mental to-do list, then quickly got off the phone.

In addition to the hard liquor, the bar's minirefrigerator was also stocked with Chinese and domestic beers and several current brands of water. Next to the bar, a large buffet table had been laid out to display the gourmet snacks, upon which starving mah-jongg players were wont to nibble.

Yes, I know it could be effectively argued that Chinese Chicken Salad was hardly an authentic Asian recipe. But please remember whom we serve. Our party guests were the denizens of L.A., after all, and like all of the city's thin and hip, they were serious salad junkies. No Southern California caterer would go broke pandering to this city's intense cravings for mass quantities of gourmet roughage and bottled water.

I checked out Holly's finished salad, rearranged the golden chopsticks, and admired a few of the other bowls and platters. An abundance of fresh fruit, sliced and beautifully arranged, was heaped on a large ornate Chinese platter. Amid Buster Dubin's valuable Chinese carvings and his astonishing collection of Chinese magic gizmos, the display looked perfect.

This is it for me: this brink of high adventure, this special time of fresh expectation, of careful preparations completed, this greedy anticipation of pleasures to come. I love this time right before the party begins. Everything clean and ready, everything beautiful and expectant.

In this brief pause before show time, I was alone. Ray had stepped outside, no doubt to grab a smoke. Back in the kitchen, Wes was beginning to prepare the dim sum with Holly's assistance.

Footsteps echoed up the hallway. I am pretty good at recognizing gaits and footfalls. Call it a little-appreciated talent. So, expecting Wes, I turned.

Lieutenant Chuck Honnett walked into the room.

"I told them I'd find you." He stood in the doorway to the party room and gave me a look that was almost a smile.

My heart did a funny little half gainer with a twist. I was actually a little annoyed with my heart. I guess that's why they call it an involuntary muscle.

"Honnett." It was not my most original opening.

"From what?"

"And you think I'm an idiot for giving her money so she could get a decent night's rest."

"No. I think you are a good friend."

"Well, she's not my friend, actually," I said, feeling uncomfortable.

"You're a good person, then." Honnett had blue eyes. Deep, deep blue. "But I'm not sure why you have to get yourself mixed up in stuff all the time."

He stood there, across the party room, looking at me, trying to figure me out. Well, that might take the man quite a while. I stared back. Honnett had the look of a transplanted Texas man, just off the range, with that sort of outdoor skin and long legs that look good in jeans, and the kind of hard body that came from real work, not workouts.

"So, Maddie. How've you been?"

Honnett and I had a history of botched opportunities and lousy timing. He and I had had a few possibilities, a while ago. We'd flirted up and back with pretty much nothing to show for it. Nothing ever got to the interesting point. Maybe it was because both of us were more comfortable *not* knowing each other better. Now that was a sad little thought.

Or maybe it was because I was going with another guy. Honnett's job and my relationship with Arlo were enough to cool things down. My life is forever on the verge of resembling *One Life to Live* on a bad day.

"I've got to get back to work now," I said, "if you're sure there's nothing that can be done."

"No. The problem you had on Third Street is being handled by Santa Monica, so there's nothing to do there." His eyes squinted. "And your friend, McBride, if you'll pardon me saying this, sounds pretty flaky."

"Yeah. But you know, her husband was a big star. And he died not too long ago. Something may be weird about that."

"There are lots of old stars in this town. Some of them die. We can't go digging one up just because something he owned goes and gets itself snatched and his ex-wife is feeling antsy. Right?"

to ask Buster who does his housecleaning. She's exception-
ally thoro . . ."

Holly looked at me with her big puppy-dog eyes. I read
pity. "Even if you don't want to admit it, there is a percepti-
ble level of hormone residue left in this room."

She makes me laugh. What can I say?

"Look, I know he's a cop and all . . ." she began.

"Yes?"

"On the other hand, Honnett's the kind of a cop who
doesn't have to wear a uniform, which you figure makes his
whole copness a little easier to take."

On the expensive sound system, Ash's version of "Kung
Fu Fighting" was coming to a close. And then, in the brief
silence that followed, I heard three muted mellow musical
tones coming from the front of the house.

"Ah."

The doorbell meant that our party guests were about to
arrive.

slipped away, followed by murmurs of "Thanks, man," and "These Slings are gonna get me in trouble."

The party was warming up, and I was satisfied. I, too, have gotten rather hooked on the game of mah-jongg since I've been catering the Club's social nights, and I perched on the corner of a nearby sofa to watch Buster's table set up their wall.

In preparation for the new hand, each player began to build a line. As they gossiped, Verushka and Trey and Buster and Quita reached forward into the array of shuffled, face-down tiles, and selected random pairs, stacking them in neat bundles of twos, and pulling the bundles back until they clacked against the edge of each of their mah-jongg racks. In this way, each player began constructing his or her own row of tiles two high and eighteen across. When these lines were completed, all four players pushed their racks forward, forming a cream-colored square made up of double-high rows of tiles. The wall.

"Buster is still East," Quita said. She gazed at Buster from under heavily made-up lids and pulled the little green umbrella from out of her drink.

East Wind was a favored position in mah-jongg. In every round, each player gets a turn to be East, which gives him or her several scoring advantages. He may keep the East position only so long as he continues to have winning hands. Once another player goes mah-jongg, the Winds shift, as it were, and the player to his right becomes East.

The whole symbolism of this game is rather fascinating.

Buster looked up at me and grinned. "We ever gonna get you to join in the fun, Madeline?"

"Not if you are still playing for a dollar a point."

"Madeline. Darling. You're a rich caterer. You charge exorbitant fees. You can afford to indulge in life's upscale pleasures."

"Honey, leave her alone." Quita took a slow sip of her Sling. "She's not interested in gambling with lunatics like you, she's interested in cooking."

Quita was getting on my nerves.

Then, in a flurry of excitement, a young woman's voice

"Oh. Sorry."

Quita wasn't paying strict attention. After the wall of tiles is formed, there are very specific rules as to where the wall is broken to begin dealing out the tiles. "I don't know why we have to do it this way. Why does East throw the dice and then we count around to see where the wall gets opened up anyway?"

"To preserve a romantic Chinese tradition, my love." Buster took one of her hands in his.

Quita giggled and glanced over at Trey.

"And to prevent cheating," Trey said, looking up at her.

Quita quickly picked up the dice and threw a four.

"Four plus eight is twelve," Trey offered helpfully.

"I know that." Quita laughed and counted, brushing her finger lightly over the tops of the tiles from the left hand side of the wall in front her until she reached "12." She lifted up that pair of tiles and placed them on top of the tiles to the left of the break.

I stood up to check on the other tables of guests. They were all deeply engaged in the tiles and the conversation. At one table, small, colorful gaming chips were exchanged, as the latest winning hand demanded its monetary reward.

"Hey, Madeline. Don't you want to hear about Noah?"

I turned back to my host. "Of course I do. I thought you were concentrating on your game."

"Talk to him. Please." Verushka drawled the last word out, begging. "Distract him. Keep his mind off the game. He's already stolen $50 from me. I need help!"

I reperched on the edge of the white damask sofa, always delighted to mix and mingle with the guests, when my clients preferred. As this was a long-standing gig of ours, Wes and I had become especially casual with Buster and his regulars at the Sweet and Sour.

"Now listen up." Buster hushed his rowdy friends, including four women sitting at the table beside him. "Madeline asked why the East Wind position is so significant in the game and I was telling her about Noah. *East* had been the prevailing wind during the great storm that caused the Great Flood."

hallway in Heather's grandma's house. In the late evenings, we were expected to be up in Heather's yellow room, if not sleeping, then at least in bed, giggling, gossiping, and hiding our laughter under the sunflower comforters. But on Friday nights, we used to make a break for it. We would sneak to the top of the steps, careful not to make the top one squeak, to watch her grandmother play maj with the gals. At ten years old, we were preteen Mata Haris.

I remember those nights with such fondness. Heather and I would hide in the darkness, sitting still in our long Lanz flannel nighties on the top step, just out of eyesight of Rose Lieberman and the mah-jongg ladies. We'd eavesdrop, listening to the older women laugh and mildly swear to the accompaniment of the swift and expert clicking of the tiles. I remembered catching whiffs of Chanel No. 5. I remember the flicker of the Sterno candle, which was lit beneath Rose's polished silver chafing dish, its task to keep warm the cocktail weenies in a thick sweet barbecue sauce. I remember feeling safe among the nearby sounds of adult female camaraderie.

"Dead hand." Verushka pushed back her chair. The others at her table grumbled that Buster would remain East and began, again, to shuffle the tiles.

At the door to the game room, right on schedule, Holly arrived with the Dim Sum cart, ready to begin serving. We had discussed with Dubin earlier the possibility of serving an authentic Chinese banquet, but he resisted. He didn't want to slow down the MJ action with a heavy meal. And we agreed Dim Sum would suit the crowd nicely, despite the unconventional hour. The custom of offering bite-size morsels known as Dim Sum started in teahouses in China as a pre-lunch thing. But we were rather nonconformist in our food tastes at the Sweet and Sour Club.

Dim Sum was a popular treat, and the players looked up from their hands and chattered with excitement when they spotted Holly and her cart.

Dubin was the sort of man who fully enjoyed himself at his own events. Seated at the game table, he found Holly's exposed waistline was but a foot or so from his nose.

I winked at Holly. She didn't notice. Instead, she stole a few seconds to blow her bangs back up off her sweaty brow.

As I moved around the room, following Holly's path, serving the dipping sauces and helping Ray pass out plates and chopsticks, I noticed the gamers' reaction to our little "heart's delights." There were comments on this one, and compliments on that one. The Turnip Cake was admired and sampled, as each of the evening's players listened to the story of its portent of good fortune. All in all, a successful event.

I moved to the back of the room to help clear up some empty metal Dim Sum tins. As I approached a far table, I couldn't help but overhear a conversation between Verushka and a man I hadn't met before. He looked to be in his mid-thirties, which of course meant he was probably closer to forty-five, using Hollywood math.

I guess I had half expected to overhear some additional raves over the evening's cuisine. The man, wearing black everything, bent his head close to Verushka, and said, "Okay. Just get it back to me, right?"

"You know I'm good for it," she said, and then looked up with a start, noticing at last that I was standing there.

My eyes, however, were instantly focused on a twentysomething couple. Kelli, the daughter of that Channel 2 news anchorman, and Bo, the beach volleyball champion who did all those Miller commercials. Their passion was, uh, aflame. They were, in fact, making out with such enthusiasm that I could hardly interrupt to ask them if they'd care for another round of steamed octopus balls. But most of my immodest staring at the beautiful couple in the lip lock was camouflage. I hoped Verushka might decide that I hadn't overheard her conversation, after all.

Party planners have a few too many plates to keep spinning to get really involved in the party guests. We have plenty to worry about and a lot of things to hope for. And added to the hope that the Dim Sum wouldn't get too sticky, and the hope that we'd brought enough Chinese soda, and the hope that Holly wouldn't faint from the heat of her steaming cart before we'd finished the meal service, I now fervently

Chapter 11

I love to plan. I love to cook. I love to party. But I love the relaxing close of a party almost as much. It was eleven o'clock. Dim Sum had been finished hours ago. Many hot mah-jongg hands had been played. We were almost finished clearing away dessert dishes. Our daringly retro Chinese Fireworks Bombe, an amazing bowl-shaped dessert, had been a showy success. Even Trey, who had a nasty habit of ignoring the food, was impressed. He noticed the auspicious number of seven lit sparklers and gave me a less than cynical smile.

The party was winding down. Coffee drinks had been served and refilled. Some of the guests had begun packing up their personal mah-jongg sets. Others were sitting around, lazily nursing their cappuccinos.

Wes, Ray, and I were finished cleaning up Buster Dubin's small kitchen, and I told Ray to go home, counting out the money I owed him in cash, apologizing for coming up a little short. I told him to come by the next afternoon, Thursday, and I'd have the twenty-five I still owed him.

"No problem." Ray showed a lot of straight, white teeth. "Dubin peeled me a C."

I smiled. The art of tipping is yet another of Buster's many talents. I looked over at Holly, who was semicollapsed on a kitchen chair. "Are you okay, pumpkin?"

Holly was sprawled upon the kitchen table. Without lifting her head from the crook of her bent elbow, upon which it

able tasty artificial colors and chemicals, it was the bubbly antidote to whatever ailed me.

There was a knock at the back door. The black poodle dog, whose tail wagged off the seconds on the wall above the sink, displayed the time: 11:10.

"Must be Lee." I opened the kitchen door and there she stood.

"Hi, Maddie. I hope I am not late." Lee Chen stood on the threshold, carrying a mah-jongg case. She was tiny, the size who spent a lifetime shopping in the "petite" section, down in the extremely low numbers. At a guess, I'd say she had to be in her sixties. Her short, jet-black hair and her smooth skin did not give away her age, but I had known her long enough to hear her tell about her twin granddaughters at Stanford.

I gave her a hug. At five feet five inches, I almost felt tall. "How are you tonight, Lee?"

"I feel wonderful, Maddie dear." Lee Chen was educated in Hong Kong, and her accent was faintly British.

Holly attempted to lift her head, revealing a face that had been steam-cleaned of all makeup. "Hi, Lee."

"Hello there, Holly. Is something wrong? You look very pale."

"She served dim sum tonight," I explained. "She'll recover."

"Dim sum is a special treat." Lee smiled at Holly and turned back to me. "It turned out very well, Maddie?"

"Yes, thanks to a wonderful teacher I had a few years ago."

In fact, I had studied Chinese cooking with Lee Chen. After years of running her own popular restaurant, she taught a master's class in Cantonese cuisine at UCLA Extension for just one quarter, and I was lucky enough to get in.

Lee had an interesting past. She spent much of her childhood in the city of Canton, now called Guangzhou. She was full of stories about her visits with Ling Ah, her mother's sister. In addition to passing down family recipes, Auntie Ling Ah also taught Lee about Confucius. What Lee learned as a girl in her auntie's kitchen became lessons she shared with us. Her course was the most spiritual and serene cooking class I can remember taking.

fer to do mah-jongg tile readings moved the party into a second peak of excitement. One by one, the players sat with Lee at a little table near the fireplace. One by one, she instructed them to shuffle the tiles facedown and select thirteen. Most were very happy with Lee's predictions.

Verushka would hear good news about money soon, Lee foresaw. Verushka, naturally, was happy to hear that. In more startling news, Trey and the Swansons could expect a visit from the stork. This news pleased Max and Greta Swanson silly. They were a cute couple. But the stork news left Trey shaking his tousled blond bachelor head. Oh, well. Can't please 'em all.

Most of the others eagerly listened to predictions of the future with that great L.A. mixture of hope and skepticism. Each took a turn to learn that: a new game-show pilot would be picked up, a Silverlake band would find a label, a new job involving both water and costumes (!) was around the corner, a health problem (having to do with feet) was to be overcome, a canned-fruit voice-over job was a sure thing, a location would send one to Brazil, a bad agent would be lost and a lost Gucci bag was to be found (look in high places), a prestigious preschool would have a last-minute opening for twins, a ski accident was to be averted in Aspen, a new sports car should be ordered in the auspicious color of red, a script needed a quick rewrite, a beach house would have termite damage, beware, and a network would be unfaithful. Well, that last went without saying. By midnight, the only ones whose fortune had yet to be read were the hosts.

Buster had just said good-bye to the last of the guests. Quita watched Trey as he walked out with Verushka. She said, "Doesn't it look like Verushka's gaining weight?"

That has to be the single most catty comment I'd heard after a party. I was annoyed, but I ignored it. Instead, I called to Buster, "Come on over here, with your lucky red jacket. Your future awaits. Your turn."

"Oh, goodie." Buster loped over, then slouched down in the chair opposite Lee Chen and grinned. He looked across the room and noticed Quita down by the mirrored bar, serving herself another Singapore Sling from a pitcher Ray had

"You had good luck tonight. You won a big pot of money, I think."

Quita McBride looked up from the bar. She walked, a little unsteadily, over to join us. "That's an easy guess," Quita said softly. "Look at how the man is gloating. I'd say it was shocking bad manners for the host of the party to take so much money from his friends."

"I don't think it is his fault, Miss," Lee said, laughing. "He cannot avoid fate, you see? He is East Wind, tonight."

"That is so true," Buster said. "I can't help it if I'm lucky."

Quita sat down on Buster's lap and turned to Lee Chen. "So how does all this fortune-telling work?"

"Mah-jongg, you know, is a very old game. Quite old. In China, some women play this game all day long. The men gamble in the mah-jongg halls, and even in public. The tiles, you see, have pictures and numbers engraved on the front to mark the different suits, like these." She quickly turned over a few tiles, and pulled out a tile with six stalks of bamboo, etched in green. "This one here is Six Bamboo, or sometimes in this country you say Six Bam, do you not?"

"Yes," Quita said, watching intently. "My husband taught me to play."

"Oh. This gentleman is your husband?"

"No," Quita said quickly. "Buster and I aren't married. My husband died last year. You've heard of Richard McBride, the actor?"

Little Lee Chen looked up astonished. The name of a big-time movie star has power. It's always been that way.

"Ah," Lee said, her voice recovering, "then you must know about all the tiles. The three main suits are Bamboo, Wan, and Circles."

"We call those Bam, Crack, and Dots," Buster said.

"Yes. And there are also the Flowers and the Four Winds and the Four Seasons and the three colors of Dragons. But, when I tell fortunes, the tiles become an oracle to interpret the future. Each tile in the set has a symbolic meaning all its own."

"Kind of like tarot cards," Quita said.

Lee said, "An oracle requires an interpreter if the meaning

tiles towards the South sector. Finally, he was told to push the one remaining tile toward the center.

We looked on as he completed building the pattern as he was instructed.

North 7-8-9

West 4-5-6   center tile   1-2-3 East

South 10-11-12

"Now, I turn them over in order," she told us, smiling. "And we shall see what fortune has in store for you." She turned over the center tile. "The tile in the center represents the focus of the reading. This is your present problem."

"Funny," Buster said, "it doesn't look like you, Queets."

Quita stood directly behind Buster's chair, brooding. She did not laugh.

Lee Chen studied the tile. It had a small numeral four in green and a squiggly blue Chinese character that meant four on top and a red squiggle that represented the Wan suit. "You see? It is the Four Wan, which represents the Chinese character: *Ch'in*. This character is symbolized by the lute and represents the performing arts. It is a symbol of music."

"You are unreal, Mrs. Chen," Buster said, delighted.

"My god." Quita looked at Buster. "Did you waste your question on the stupid *Warp* music video?" She turned to us, and added, "He's desperate to do it. I don't know why. But they are not coming up with the contract."

Buster gave his girlfriend a pained look. "They want me, Quita. Look at my Four Wan. They just have to come up to my price. But with my East Wind and my Four Wan, I think it's a done deal."

Then he turned back to Lee. "Please, Mrs. Chen, go on."

She continued to turn over tiles and tell their significance, but just at that moment my cell phone rang. I moved out of range of the reading so I wouldn't disturb them as I answered

up here, so many plots"—he tapped his temple—"she doesn't have much time to knock two rational thoughts together."

"I guess," I said. "I think maybe she hasn't gotten over her husband's death yet."

"She was really freaking out," Wes said, remembering like I did how differently Quita had behaved back at the Wetherbee house.

"She's a sweet kid," Buster said, "but she has problems. Hey, who doesn't?" He got up and pulled out the chair opposite Lee. "Come on, now, Maddie. Your turn."

"Don't you think we should be going?" I asked, looking off in the direction Quita had gone.

"No way. She'll keep."

"Come sit down, Madeline," Lee instructed, and so I did.

After a rapid bout of shuffling tiles, and making a lake, I quickly selected thirteen tiles and pulled them into the center. Then, as Lee guided me, I set up the tiles, three apiece in the positions that represented East, West, North, and South, and one in the center.

Lee turned over the tile in the center first.

"Ah. Six Wan. Very interesting."

"What?" I looked down at the tile. It showed the number etched in red in the upper corner and the same Chinese character as the other wan tiles etched in black.

"It means many things. One thing is intelligence."

"Of course." Wes began to laugh. "That's perfect, Mad."

"I love smart women," Buster said. "So why don't I ever date any?" He gave me a goofy look, raising his eyebrows several times, Groucho Marx style, to signify possible future romance.

I laughed and turned back to Lee. "Intelligence. That's a nice compliment, Lee. That's safe. But I forgot to think of a question. So does that botch the reading?"

Lee was intently studying the Six Wan tile. When she realized she'd been addressed she looked up quickly and smiled. "No, no. Nothing is ruined. You may have a general reading, Madeline dear. Listen and learn about the future."

She turned over another tile. Five Wan meant house. I thought perhaps it could be Wesley's new house, but she

man in life," Lee said, looking over all thirteen exposed tiles. "Stable, happy partners."

"Thank goodness," Wesley said.

"You get married soon to Arlo, Madeline?" Lee asked, after careful thinking.

"No!"

"Well," Lee said with a shy smile, pointing to the two flower tiles, "then what are these two babies doing here?"

We all laughed.

Lee said, "They are only tiles, after all. You like to hear more?"

"Go ahead." I never take this sort of thing seriously. It's just fun to imagine life's possibilities.

"Your man. He is very powerful. A very passionate person. A very affectionate man. It says this quite clearly in the tiles."

I burst out laughing. "Lee Chen!" This was not the type of reading I expected from a grandmother of twin college girls. "Really."

She joined me laughing. "I do not make this up, Maddie. You can see it yourself. Here, here, and here." She pointed out tiles as if I could read their meanings.

"Well, I'm shocked," I said, trying not to smile, kidding my former teacher.

"I do not see why you are so modest, Madeline. You know about the philosopher Kao Tzu, I think."

Buster and I shook our heads, but Wesley looked up, alert. "Kao Tzu. Yes, the famous Warring States-period philosopher."

Wesley.

"Yes," Wes said, "Kao Tzu was a keen observer of human nature."

"Very good," Lee answered. "No reason to be shy about love, Madeline. Kao Tzu said, 'Appetite for food and sex is nature.' "

Well, how was one supposed to refute a Warring States philosopher? And given his philosophy, why would one want to?

It had gotten to be so late, I was anxious to get Lee home and so we left shortly afterward. Wesley left in his own car.

Chapter 12

"OH NO!"

"Man oh man."

"Oh my God. It's dead, Madeline. You killed it."

I looked at the small, sleek cell phone, ice tea dripping off its pathetically flipped open flip part. A dark watery stain formed on the pink-linen tablecloth beneath it. The thing was dead all right.

"Oops."

I don't know how it happened, really. I am not clumsy. I am actually pretty damn graceful. But I was holding Arlo's little phone for a second and it slipped and it fell and the Atlantic Ocean of ice tea kinda swallowed it up. It fell straight into his glass. I don't know how that happened.

"Okay, I'm not a technical guy. Granted, okay?" Arlo was getting agitated, as the enormity of his cellular disaster washed over him like a wave of, well, tea. "But I'm pretty sure these things don't work anymore after they have been deliberately dunked in *iced beverages*. I'm pretty sure that was in the ninety-page Ericsson instruction manual. The phone, Maddie, is dead. It is never coming back."

I handed him my napkin. "Sorry, Arlo, honey. It was a freak accident."

And then I realized. That was *it*. That was Lee Chen's prediction of an accident. It had to be. I smiled myself silly.

Arlo looked at me with suspicion as he gently patted his little gizmo.

wireless phone and patted it gently. As we crossed the room, an upscale trattoria, I looked around. Green ivy leaves were hand-painted onto the white Italian tiles that surrounded the open-hearth pizza oven, and a full-time prep chef at the counter continually chopped the ingredients to their famous Leon Chop Salad, even this late. I noticed the head of prime-time programming at NBC sitting alone in a corner booth. We had catered a large event for him last year. The hours people worked in this industry were cruel. He was absorbed in reading a script and appeared to be the only one in the room who hadn't looked up when I *accidentally* sent Arlo's little phone deep-tea diving. I decided it would be better not to disturb him. I could say hello later.

I sat down and looked over at Arlo. He was pushing and repushing a number of tiny buttons on his cell phone in frustration. Yes. I got it. It didn't work.

I had been telling Arlo about my day between his urgent calls. I told him about what happened in Santa Monica. I told him about the strange conversation at Wesley's Wetherbee house. As I started and restarted my saga, Arlo juggled calls. Momentous decisions re: series minority (Chicano vs. Asian); sofa color (Nile green vs. plum); and rehab program for the star (Sierra Tucson Clinic vs. Betty Ford) were made. And as I tried to tell Arlo about the mah-jongg party, I waited while he received three more calls during which everyone wanted to change those decisions. And then the ice tea incident occurred.

"Dead, dead, dead . . ." Arlo looked me in the eye.

Perhaps I should explain where I'm coming from. I've been going through a lot lately. Heavy things just keep happening. I mean, for a gourmet chef and caterer, admittedly a lighthearted kind of profession, I've been swimming an awful lot, lately, in the deep end of life's little pool. I have observed several serious events recently, some involving death and lives ruined. So watching Arlo make a federal case out of a little mishap with passion fruit ice tea was not playing well. I was becoming less amused, by the minute, with always having to accommodate Arlo's inalienable right as a comedy writer to milk anguish to the tenth power, so long as

in food. Nothing green. Nothing, in fact, of a vegetable nature of any kind. Imagine what the average four-year-old likes and you can safely have Arlo over for dinner.

By the time I looked back over to check on what was up with the NBC guy, he had gone.

"So, anyway, whose party did you do tonight?" Arlo asked.

"Buster Dubin. He's a neighbor of mine. Remember?" I think I'd explained this to Arlo on at least four occasions.

"What does he do again?" Arlo asked.

"Directs," I said, looking at Arlo, waiting for him to wake up. "Remember? He did the music video for The Julies. And a bunch of big commercials. You know the one for Tattoos.com? That's his."

"Oh, yeah."

"Oh, yeah."

"And isn't his girlfriend that model or something?"

I shook my head. "That was one of his old girlfriends. Lately he's been living with Quita McBride. He kinda goes through women."

"I'd better use the pay phone to call Mark back," Arlo said, checking his watch. "Before the food comes."

"I thought it might be nice if we, like, talked."

"Oh?" Arlo adjusted his glasses. "Okay. If you say so, sweetie. A talk. Shoot."

I resettled in my chair and tried to restart the evening on a better note. "I heard this lovely story yesterday. From my friend, Sophie."

"Is she still the chef at that restaurant in Pasadena?"

"Uh-huh, she's doing great. Did I tell you she's adopting a baby girl? From China. She just found out they've matched her to a little girl."

"She wants a baby?" Arlo began doing his Rodney Dangerfield schtick, pulling at the collar of his denim shirt, mock nervous. "Um." He cleared his throat. "She didn't go giving you any ideas."

"Arlo. Sophie's ten years older than I am. She's thought about this decision for a long time. Jeez! She would be a perfect mother. But don't worry. I'm not ready. You know

set on spoolies. And that's its natural state. In fact, it does take a lot of time to brush it out and blow-dry it straight, so I mostly let it go in ringlets. But I knew Arlo's schtick. He liked to disarm me with wit.

"So," he said, in conclusion, "it's really absurd to be thinking about babies."

Our waitress brought us fresh glasses of ice tea and withdrew quickly. Just what this man needed.

"Arlo. Did I say this has anything to do with us? Can you possibly imagine there are other people in the world? And sometimes, just sometimes, there are things that happen to *them*."

"Other people." Arlo sipped his drink. "Now that you mention it, I do believe I've heard of them. So go on about Sophie."

"Thank you. She is very excited about her new daughter. She had just gone to the bookstore and found some great books. One of them is a little folk tale from China. It's called *The Empty Pot*."

Arlo spoke up in a tone of voice that sounded absolutely outraged. "Now wait a darn minute. Sophie wants to be a mom and she's buying books about pot? I think some women were just not meant to be mothers."

"Arlo!"

"I'm joking. I'm joking. Go on already." I think Arlo gets a special charge out of riling me up.

"I wanted to tell you about this story because it really affected me. Okay? So settle down."

"I'm settled." He put on his good-listener face, the one that must have disarmed Mrs. Beven, his fourth-grade teacher, when he was in reality whispering one-liners to the back row, and then chuckling when they got into trouble for laughing.

But this was about the most of Arlo's attention I'd had in a while. With neither one of us at our offices, and his cell phone temporarily out of commission, I began my story. "*The Empty Pot* is a folk tale about an ancient Chinese emperor. The aging emperor gives one flower seed to each child in his kingdom. He tells them, 'In a year's time show me

She looked down at the plate, and said, "Oh." She squinted up at Arlo and looked like she was about to say something. Instead, she just turned around with his plate. It was at that moment I pushed my chair back.

"Mad? Hey! Where are you going?"

I grabbed my purse from the floor and stood up. I took one long last look at Arlo. I took it all in. His familiar funny handsome face. His tousled hair. His mouth. His wide shoulders beneath his designer blue-denim shirt. His slim waist, zipped into expensive jeans. His long, slender fingers with their nibbled fingernails. His Rolex. His "I ♥ El Lay" key ring with the keys to his Porsche. His dead cell phone.

I turned and walked away.

"Hey, Mad. What's going on? Madeline!" Arlo had raised his voice a notch, getting the attention of just about everyone in the semifilled room.

I had made it about ten feet before I stopped and turned. "I just realized something. I've been with the wrong guy. I don't need a guy with an Emmy and an ulcer. I need someone who can bring me an empty pot."

"Madeline. That's nuts."

"Not to me." I walked back to our table, flushing hot. I stood there, looking down upon him. Seeing him now. "Arlo. I want different things than you do, that's all. I don't know what took me so long to realize it. I just need something else."

"You want kids? Is that it? You think you want a baby?"

"NO! I don't want a baby!" I shouted. "I want honesty. That's what that story was about, you moron! I want a little freaking honesty from the man I love."

I looked up and realized everyone in the place had just clammed up, watching Arlo and me. Our waitress stood off to one side, holding the plate with Arlo's hamburger and its new, de-seeded bun.

"I want an honest man, Arlo. I am in serious need of an honest individual who can eat a freaking hamburger with the works."

"Mad. What exactly is going on here? First you drown my cell phone, then you insult my burger. Are you trying to tell

Riverside and Yucca was a fairly busy one. Even with the early-morning light traffic, I expected such an unsteady tot to have an adult by the hand.

The little black flare-legged pants got to me. I looked down at my own clothes. I had come straight from the Sweet and Sour Club party. I was still dressed in white V-neck tank top and black flare-leg pants.

The little girl tottered all the way to the corner, and I was beginning to feel a tiny ripple of alarm shoot up the back of my neck. The child, perhaps twelve months old, looked over to where I stood, sixty feet up the sidewalk.

"Hi!" I started walking toward her and she stood stock-still, big almond-shaped eyes fastened on mine.

What was she doing out here at night, anyway? Don't babies go to sleep earlier than this? Shouldn't she have a parent looking after her? As I slowly came closer she looked back down the side street, toward the spot beyond my vision where I presumed her adult must have been standing. I was just about to reach her at the corner and get a look down the side street. I felt like yelling a little at the idiot who would leave a baby alone so long on a major street corner.

The child had big, very dark eyes. Her deep bangs covered her forehead like thick, shiny fringe. As I approached, she backed up a few faltering steps, almost backing off the curb.

"Wait there, honey," I said, in that singsong cartoon voice people use to talk to babies, an octave above normal speech. "Wait, wait, wait . . ." I crooned to her, as she teetered on the edge of the foot-high sidewalk curb.

Just when I needed it most, it became clear that I was lacking a vital rescue skill. I just don't have that squeaky-voice thing down. Without friends who have babies, I've never practiced. Who knew it would be such a drawback? Shit!

"Wait there . . ."

The child took one more baby step backward. In an instant she tumbled down into the street.

"NO!"

I watched her fall, heard her cry out, and then I looked up.

Chapter 13

*S*ometimes you have to believe in fate.

You don't want to, of course. You want to be modern and cynical and scientific—that is, if, like me, you'd been raised by rational, unromantic parents in the Midwestern suburbs. As life goes on, if things occasionally seem odd and even a bit overly coincidental, you don't wig out and go all Mulder. You remind yourself about laws of probability and mathematics and odds. You want to believe in randomness, in one-out-of-a-bazillion chances, in luck. But then sometimes, maybe when you are least expecting it, like when you are standing on some odd Burbank street corner, hugging a little girl you hadn't known existed only moments earlier, some unsettling "fateful" thoughts may come to mind. At such a moment, you might start to lose a bit of your Scully cool.

What if?

What if, say, I had not gone out to dinner. What if I had not dropped a particular object (blue Ericsson X12) into a particular drink (large, full, just Sweet 'n Low'd)? What if I had not told Arlo good-bye, and walked out before tasting my Leon Chop Salad with chicken, what then? Was every choice, every decision, and every act leading to that one moment at the curb? Does all the stuff, both good and bad, that happens to us in our seemingly random lives nudge us in a very specific direction?

The baby I was holding in my arms began to settle down. My heart was still pumping hard. My hair felt damp with

and getting loud, you know. I didn't want to wake her up. I just walked around the block to finish it. When I came back around the corner, I heard the noise over here. I had no idea Caroline was involved. How could I have known she would . . . ?" There were tears in his eyes. ". . . that she wouldn't be safe?"

"Well, she's okay." I said, feeling the energy sap out of my limbs. "She's okay now." People do dumb things. It happens. And who ever expects such danger waits on a quiet night like this?

"I know you," he said, as the sound of a police siren wailed in the distance, growing louder. "You did a party. You're . . ." He shook his head.

"Madeline Bean."

"Yes." He looked at me again and then he looked at the smashed truck perched awkwardly up on the sidewalk. "I will never forget this."

I felt a little weak. I looked for Arlo among the small crowd, but he wasn't there.

"I'll never forget this," the father said. "Never. I'm . . . Can I do something for you? I mean to thank you?"

"Why don't you take a little time off work?" I suggested.

The baby began to close her eyes, her head heavy on his shoulder. He shifted her in his arms so she'd be in a more comfortable position.

"I'm going to quit."

"You are?"

"I have never been so sure of any decision in my life."

I nodded and told him, good for you, but I knew. It was only the fear talking. He had made a mistake that almost couldn't be taken back. But in time, in a few hours or a few days, he'd remember his other fears—the payments due on his BMW and his mortgage and his MasterCard. He'd be overcome again with the fear that the network's new pilots were crap, or that the fall season would tank and someone would figure out that programming executives like him were just gamblers, guessing and playing for time.

And yet. Wait. I was beginning to see past my pat, cynical

Chapter 14

"This is not a good time, Honnett." I sat myself down next to him on the step, settling my purse on the step below.

"Too late for you? I thought you were the tough girl. Nothing is too late for Madeline Bean. What happened to that?"

"That is a very good question." I didn't look at him. Sitting together on the step in the chill air, our sides touching, the warmth of his body felt good.

"Rough night?" he asked, checking me out. "You kinda lost your zip."

"You have that keen detective talent for observation working, don't you?" I said. "I have indeed lost my zip. Please don't let it get out, though. Bad for business."

"What's the matter?" Honnett's voice got husky. He usually sounded more, I don't know—cynical.

"I'm tired, maybe," I said, trying to get my voice to sound lighter. "My birthday's coming, did you know that?"

"You're feeling old?" He began to laugh. "You're like a puppy. What are you turning? Thirty? I don't even own jeans anymore from back when I was thirty."

"Yeah, it does sort of cheer me up to hang out with an old guy like you," I said, beginning to smile. I looked up at him. Big mistake. Honnett looked especially good in street lamplight. Wouldn't you know?

"I'm trying to cheer you up, here. Is it working?" He kind of whispered. My tiny street was deserted, and we were sit-

My house was built at a time when the famed tile-maker was doing relief tiles in colors popular with the Arts and Crafts movement, like gold and moss green. My fireplace surround was covered in a rare shade of matte blue. I was mildly surprised a guy like Chuck Honnett would know anything about ceramic artists of the early twentieth century.

"Would you like me to make a fire?" he asked.

See, everything he said seemed to make me cry more. I don't have to explain, do I, that Arlo didn't know anything about building a fire. That if you couldn't turn a little metal key in the wall, Arlo was worthless. I thought about that some more as Honnett started arranging a few logs.

"I broke up with Arlo tonight. Remember him?"

"Sure. The rich kid."

I laughed. I don't know if it was hearing Arlo called "rich" or a "kid." So, Honnett thought I dated rich guys. Is that why he'd fought the attraction all these months? And the age thing again. Honnett was forty-three, I guessed, and he had told me once before he thought he was too old for me.

"That all you're gonna say?" I asked, looking at him as he lit a match and touched it to the crumpled newspaper in the grate.

"Well, from the look of you tonight, I'd have to say you aren't all that happy about losing him."

"I didn't lose him, Honnett. I walked out on him, and I'm glad I did it."

There are two wonderful wing chairs in my small upstairs living room, but he didn't choose to sit in either of them. The cushions on the down-filled sofa sank as he joined me there. "So, tell me about it."

I turned to him, made eye contact, and spoke. "I thought I loved him, Honnett. I think I still do." Tears. "When I started dating Arlo, I was getting pretty successful. The business was taking off. Wes and I had turned a corner, and I could see it. And Arlo was just as ambitious. We were the same that way."

"Oh, I think not," Honnett said, reaching up to touch my hair, pushing it back off of my wet face.

I leaned against him and talked. I told him about how I'd

"You are?" Honnett cracked a smile. "Finally, we're talking about me. Hot damn."

"Don't distract me, please. I'm thinking it all over. I think being tough and cynical has helped me become better at business."

"Yes. And seeing things from a distance, it helps you get to the truth."

"Yes." I sat back, considering the price I pay for those benefits. I have lost, I realized, that idiotic inner child everyone in L.A. is always rattling on about. I felt tears well up again. What was happening? First I go all weak on the idea of fate, and now I was crying over my inner child.

"I think . . ." I grabbed another tissue. ". . . I think I've been living in Los Angeles too long."

Honnett smiled. "Just recognizing that, Madeline, is like your armor against it."

"I want to be different. I want to be freer." I wadded up the tissue and threw it into the wastebasket.

"Then do it."

"It doesn't just go away. I still think I see everyone's ulterior motives and moves."

"For instance . . . ?" He looked over at me, and pushed one of my unruly curls back off my forehead, again.

"For instance. What do you get for being such a decent guy tonight? What is your reward?"

"Well." He looked at me again. "That fine questioning mind of yours is what would have made you a pretty good cop." And then he smiled. "I think, if you are okay now, I had better get going."

And in that moment, I knew I wanted him to stay.

I was in the shower the next morning when I thought I heard the phone ring. I stood under the oversize chrome showerhead, the old-fashioned kind that made me feel like I was rinsing shampoo out of my hair in a steamy hot downpour.

There was a tap at the bathroom door, and then I heard it open.

"What?" I looked at the bed, which just about filled my tiny room, and smiled. "I thought you had to go to work."

"I do. Please, sit down for a minute. There's something I have to tell you."

I sat down, not knowing what to expect. Now, the old Madeline Bean would have become worried, suspicious. That other Maddie would suspect the sorry, I can't have a relationship with you letdown talk. I'm afraid a lot of that old Maddie was still in charge.

"What is it? What's wrong?"

"That last call. It was the watch commander. There's been a death. I have to go."

That was it? So he wasn't letting me down easy? I felt relief, and then, shocked at myself, guilt.

"Madeline, listen. It's some bad news. I wish I didn't have to tell you this, especially this morning. You know the victim."

"What? No."

This was my punishment for one night of self-indulgence. This was why we shouldn't break up with our boyfriends who are pretty decent to us and go instantly to bed with some cop. "Who is it?"

"The woman at the party last night. Quita McBride. She fell down the steps to that big house up on the hill where you catered the party."

drawer, I think. I looked at my desk and noticed that my computer wasn't turned on. Ah, well.

"Maddie, honey, you are scaring me. What happened? Where's Wesley?"

"I don't know. I called and left a message for him. He's probably at the Wetherbee house, and his cell phone must be off."

"Something is wrong. What happened last night after I left Buster's party?"

"What happened?" I repeated, trying to think how I could explain. "I told Honnett there was something wrong. I told him I was worried. And he told me to just forget about it, Holly. He didn't think there was any real threat."

Holly drummed her long, slender fingers on the section of her baggy white capri pants that covered her knee. "I need to hear the whole thing," she said. "And then we can freak together, okay?"

I told her about the night before. At some point in the story, between the part where I broke up with Arlo Zar and the part where I saved some stranger's baby, Wesley joined us. He sat in his desk chair and didn't say a word.

"So you saved weird Curt Newton from NBC's baby girl?" Wes said, shaking his head in wonder. Both he and Holly made no comment on the part of the tale where I walked out on Arlo at La Scala Presto. I suppose they were a little gun-shy. They had been through a lot of on again/off again with us over the past six months. I realized I had taken Arlo back several times too many. They just didn't realize that we were now completely off. Instead they were going over the part with the truck crashing on the sidewalk inches from me. "So you must have been pretty scared."

"It was weird," I said, answering Wesley. "What was I doing out there on that street corner? And then that little girl. She shouldn't have been there either. What can it all mean?"

"Freak coincidence," Wesley said, thinking about it.

"Or destiny," Holly suggested.

I rubbed my head, not wanting to admit that I was getting to be more like Holly each day. "So . . . you two have noth-

"You must have been a wreck after the Arlo thing, and then that car accident thing," Holly said.

"Yes, but it was okay, Hol. I needed to cry. I felt like I awoke something inside of me that I've been missing."

"Like you awoke your *inner child*, Madeline." Holly proclaimed.

"Yes. Well." I felt suddenly squirmy. "I was hoping to avoid mentioning that disgusting concept, but maybe so."

Wesley fought back a smile. He was such a thoughtful soul.

Holly said, matter of fact, "You got in touch with your inner child and let her out. Amazing. But then Honnett was around, and who knew your inner child was starving for affection and had such amazingly poor impulse control?"

"Please. Don't remind me." I shivered.

"Well, so what's everyone so glum about?" Wes asked. "Honnett's not a terrible guy. I hope."

I smiled at Wes. "It's not that, Wesley. There's more."

They both looked at me.

"I should have been paying better attention to everyone else's needs after all. I picked a hell of a night to start getting selfish."

"Why?"

"Because Quita McBride was asking for help last night. Remember, Wes? At the Wetherbee house? She was going on about being scared, and she asked me to help her. And I said no. I thought she was nuts, which she may have been, but I said no, here's some money."

"Everyone asks you to help them, Maddie," Holly said, dismissing it. "You can't help everyone."

"Well, she seemed fine at the party later," Wes said, looking at me, worried. "Don't you think she may have been overly dramatic, Mad?"

"I don't know. I just don't know. Because even though I warned Honnett that Quita was scared and I warned him something might be going on with her, he did nothing to help. He said there was nothing the police could do."

"So?" Holly looked worried too.

can't take care of everyone. Don't do this to yourself. And anyway, it could have been an accident."

"It could, Maddie," Holly said.

"It seems like an obscene coincidence, I know," Wes said. "But coincidences happen."

I looked at him sadly.

I knew in my heart that my dear friends meant well. I knew they were worried about me. Anyone could see that I'd had quite an emotional day and night. But I was sure there was more I could do. I had to do it really. Because I was convinced that the death of Quita McBride was tied to the mahjongg set that had been found and then stolen. Or tied to the missing red book she had wanted so badly.

I was sure whatever had frightened her there at the Wetherbee house was tied to it. Maybe, even, the death of old Dickey McBride was part of what happened to Quita. Perhaps, I was afraid even to think it, Buster Dubin was involved as well.

I knew I would have to find out. I couldn't help myself. I always needed to know. I needed to know a lot more before I could begin to forgive myself for casually writing off a woman I hadn't liked very much.

One night of inner child indulgence, and now I was overwhelmed by the sting of consequences. I guess I didn't feel that hot about what I had been doing with Honnett on the night Quita McBride fell to her death.

"Yeah, aren't we both. We'll work on the neighbors and talk to friends, see if we can catch Dubin lying. Maybe I should write this down, Madeline. You left the house when?"

"Around twelve-forty-five," I said. "I don't know if Quita was still there. She'd left the game room about fifteen minutes earlier. And I told you before, she had been acting weird. She told me she was going to spend the night in a hotel."

"Did she tell you which one?" Honnett asked.

"No."

"I'll look into it. If she checked in somewhere and then came back to Dubin's house, we can trace her through credit cards."

I shook my head. "I lent her some cash. She would have used cash."

Honnett looked up. "It's a long shot anyway," he said. "She probably never left the house."

"So you don't know anything," I said.

"I've talked with several of the party guests already. I'll talk to the rest of them today and tomorrow, if I can. They haven't told us much. The neighbors have been a little more helpful. Time of death seems to be near 3:00 A.M. A neighbor heard some noise at five minutes past. Woke him up. Sounded like trash cans falling. Her body was found among four large plastic trash bins down at the end of the driveway by the street. That fits with the time we get from the coroner."

"How did she die, Honnett? Exactly," I asked.

"I'd have to guess until the autopsy report comes back."

"Guess, then."

He looked at me. "She fell down the steps and hit her head. A lethal head injury. Blunt trauma. They'll likely find an intracranial bleed, which is bleeding in and around the brain with or without a fracture of the skull. This sort of death happens every day, Maddie. Especially when someone is 'under the influence.' Death can be instantaneous or it may take minutes, or hours, or even days."

"Will the coroner be able to tell you if Quita was pushed?" I asked.

Honnett read his notes quickly. "There was seven dollars and change in her wallet."

"I wonder what happened to the eight twenties I gave her earlier."

The waiter came to our table and delivered a pizza, putting it on one of those wire stands that held it up off the table. Honnett served himself three slices, but I wasn't hungry. I sipped a Diet Coke, wondering what to make of us now.

Honnett was polite, professional, maybe even friendly. But nothing more. I could almost believe our evening together had never happened.

"This must be hard for you, Honnett. Interviewing a woman you've been . . . you know, I don't know what to call it."

He met my eyes. "I guess you're angry with me."

So he was a good detective, after all. "Maybe."

Honnett let out a breath slowly. "Because I didn't call you?"

I let it just hang there.

"Or because I have this job to do? Because I'm a cop? I remember you telling me once that you don't care for cops, right?"

"How about," I said, "because you didn't take me seriously? Quita was scared. I knew she was in trouble, no matter how crazy she was acting. And what did you do about it?"

"Look. I know you feel bad."

We sat there looking at one another.

"Look, Maddie, no one is happy that a young woman fell down a flight of stairs and died, but things like that are known to happen. Hell, she'd been drinking all night. She was wearing those crazy shoes. The steps were steep. It was late."

"She was scared," I said.

"I know. I'm working on it. Neighbors saw lights on upstairs all night, so Dubin was probably awake. Some friends have told us Dubin and Quita were about to break up. That still doesn't mean the guy pushed her with intent to kill her. If we don't find a witness or some major forensic evidence, what can we do?"

"You don't strike me as a guy who lacks confidence in his job skills, Honnett."

"There are limits to this job."

"I've always said so. But if she knows about Dickey McBride's red book . . ."

"Chances are Catherine Hill knows nothing at all about the book or about Mrs. McBride and her unfortunate death. Chances are, even knowing nothing, she'll shine me on. Because people like her are into privacy. But let's just suppose for a minute that she does know something that has a bearing on our investigation. And let's suppose it's information she considers incriminating, whatever that might be. What are the chances she's going to tell me that information?"

Following the rules, burdened by the laws, he couldn't get any real information that way.

"I see."

He stood up, and said, "I'll call you when I hear anything."

"You can call me before that, too, you know."

"Aren't you coming?"

"I think I'll stay and finish my Diet Coke," I said. And figure out just how I could go about meeting the multi-Oscar-winning leading lady, Catherine Hill.

"Right." Wes looked at me with concern. "But you don't think it was an accident."

"You know, I wish I did."

Wes leaned over and patted the top of my head.

"I'd feel better," I said, "if I could be sure."

"Of course you would." He was never enthusiastic about my little investigations, but I had faced a few problems in the past and gotten through them all right.

"This is going to be useful." I touched the edge of Dickey McBride's antique rosewood mah-jongg case. It was back with us since the Santa Monica police had found too many smudged fingerprints on it and none they could identify. They hadn't seemed surprised. In all, their manner had not encouraged our expectation, either, that they might continue pursuing this crime with anything mimicking vigilance.

"So how are you going to get in touch with Catherine Hill?" Wes asked. "I'm assuming she's not in the phone book."

I had this plan. It seemed to me that I would have more success talking to Catherine Hill, privately, than the police ever would if they tried to question her officially. And that was assuming the cops were interested in Catherine Hill. Which they weren't.

But first, I had to figure out how to reach her. I knew she had a big house in Bel Air, but short of going out to Westwood and buying a Map to the Stars' Homes from one of those boys on a street corner, I was stumped as how to talk to her.

"Remember Six Degrees of Kevin Bacon?" Wes asked, starting to erase another line on his plan.

"The game? Of course."

Several years ago, a bunch of college boys with too much time on their hands and a bottle of Southern Comfort came up with the game Six Degrees of Kevin Bacon. The game is a rather inspired, if loony joke based on the John Guare play and movie *Six Degrees of Separation*, which suggests that we are all connected by six or fewer stages of acquaintance.

In other words, if I were in line at my neighborhood Mayfair market and I ran into my hairstylist friend, Germaine,

"Should I try it?" Wes asked, tapping his keyboard.

"Of course. Everybody cut footloose," I said.

Wesley was already on it. He'd entered Catherine's name into the screen, and a few seconds later he smiled.

"It's a good one. Catherine Hill was in *Rhapsody* in 1954 with Vittorio Gassman and Vittorio Gassman was in *Sleepers* in 1996 with Kevin Bacon."

"So," I said, pulling out my cell phone, "all I have to do is ask Kevin to call Gassman and explain I need to talk to Catherine Hill."

"Right," Wes said. "However, if Vittorio Gassman is still alive and if he lives anywhere we can reach him, we have to wonder if the phone number he may have for Catherine Hill is still current after almost fifty years."

"True." I began to rethink. I would hate to bother a celebrity client just to run into an eventual dead end anyway. "Besides, I need some up-to-the-minute scoopage on Ms. Hill. This won't do."

"Wow," Wes said, looking back at his computer screen.

"What?"

"Did you know Kevin Bacon is only two links away from Bob Barker?" He looked up from his screen. "Sorry, Mad. I got carried away."

I knew he was dying to tell me. "Go on."

"Bob Barker was in *Happy Gilmore* in 1996 with Andrew Johnston who . . ."

A male voice with a Spanish accent interrupted us. "Mr. Wesley?"

It was one of the men who were working on the house. Wesley put down the laptop and went over to talk to him. After a few seconds, Wes turned to me. "We've got visitors. I'll go see who it is."

Who had come to call? Maybe Honnett, I thought, and felt my pulse pick up with a jolt. Maybe he'd tracked me down and was coming with some big, important news. It was unlikely, but still . . .

Maybe Arlo, I thought, jolting in another direction. Ah, what about that? It had been a couple of days since I'd walked out on him at the restaurant. It was strange he hadn't

Wesley looked at me. Dead buffalo times made him edgy as a cat. In fact, he looked like he would rather be cleaning out cesspools.

"Why?" Verushka asked quickly. "Is that what the police think?"

I shrugged. "She just seemed so disturbed," I said. "Didn't any of you notice?"

"She seemed pretty wasted to me," Verushka said, looking over at Buster. "Quita was Buster's girlfriend, and we loved her, of course—but she was hard to really get to know."

"How did you meet her?" I asked Buster.

"Trey brought her over to the Sweet and Sour Club," Buster answered.

"Right," Trey said, sipping his lemonade. "She played MJ."

Buster looked over at me. "I wonder if I could talk to you? I called your office, and Holly said you were with Wes. We took a chance we'd find you here."

"We're like his escort service," Verushka said, clowning. "We're all attached at the hip, and my hip is, like, my biggest part." She laughed loudly.

"Can I have a moment with you, Madeline?" Buster asked.

We took the flagstone path through the rose garden and entered the French doors into the large empty living room. From another room we could hear the sound of a radio tuned to a Spanish language station. The plasterers had finished in this room and it smelled like damp cement. We settled ourselves on the long wooden step that leads up from the sunken living room into the entry hall.

"What can I do for you, Buster?" I'd selected a spot on the dusty hardwood about eighteen inches away from him, farther than I would normally have chosen to be seated from a friend. He was the same man with whom I'd goofed around two nights before. And yet it was different now. The shocking death of Quita McBride at Buster's house had rubbed off on him, raising uncomfortable questions. I was glad the crew was noisily at work in the room next door.

"I need a favor," Buster said.

"You get the truth. Ask me any question you want to."

I looked at Buster Dubin, his jet-black hair and his permanent five-o'clock shadow and his dancing eyes.

He said, "You know you want to ask me something."

My heart began pounding in an odd way. I became aware of the sound. I had to know. "Okay. I'll talk to Honnett."

"Excellent." Buster smiled up at me and edged a little closer on the step. "So now it's your turn. What do you want to know? And remember, I am a fairly eligible bachelor, I always win at MJ, and I have made a fortune on the stock market."

So Buster expected me to ask him advice? I was afraid he was in for a shock. I wanted the truth about something a lot more important to me than his sex life, or how many tech shares he was holding.

"Truth," I said, looking him in the eyes. "What really happened after I left your house?"

"After you left?" He stared at me.

"This is your game," I said.

"Quita and I had a fight."

Oh, man.

Buster told me more. "Quita was a good kid, really. But, you know, she could be demanding as hell, and lately she was getting all weird. You know, she had never seemed happy. It was like she always had some other thing on her mind. And over the past week, Quita had been getting more and more spooky. I told her she didn't have to leave right away. She could take as long as she needed to move her things."

"So you broke up with her that night?"

"Look, it's not like I was breaking her heart, okay? I'm pretty sure she was seeing someone else. I get a bad rap for going through a lot of very beautiful women, but I'm not really so difficult to please. A lot of times the chick leaves me."

Yeah, I thought. Right.

"Now look at you, there," he said, smiling. "You don't believe me. And that is terribly sweet. It is. But I guess I just wasn't famous enough or pretty enough to keep Quita's attention. I am just a humble guy who directs TV ads. I wasn't

"I'll take your message to my cop friend," I said. "He'll come back and terrorize you, though."

"That's cool. And maybe when it's all over, I can take you to Copenhagen."

cousin Maria worked for a family in Bel Air on Bellagio Road. So that's where we started and Alba got on the phone.

Her cousin Maria works with Rosa from Guatemala, and it turned out that Rosa's sister-in-law Lillian was the nanny for Catherine Hill's grandchildren. Imagine that. Lillian had the phone number for Sonia who worked days for Miss Catherine Hill. In L.A., we can play the Six Degrees game both upstairs and downstairs.

With just a few phone calls, I was speaking to Sonia, a sweet-voiced young woman with a light Spanish accent. She answered my question, telling me what time on Friday would be my best bet.

I timed my trip accordingly. I checked my watch as I drove up Bellagio Road. On either side were estates that would sell today in the two-to-ten range. That's millions. Hidden behind tall fences and large hedges were the homes that once belonged to Ray Milland and Gene Roddenberry, Franchot Tone and Jim Backus, John Forsythe and Alfred Hitchcock.

On the 11500 block, I pulled my vintage Grand Wagoneer up to a pair of tall, wrought-iron gates. They barred a long brickwork drive that led up to Catherine Hill's massive property.

I sat there in my car for a while, taking in the sounds and sights of the street. It was quiet, save the ubiquitous on/off hissing of the sprinklers. I pressed the speaker button on the gate and after a minute, a voice greeted me.

"Who is there, please?"

I was startled and thrilled at the voice. Instead of some anonymous employee, the voice that came from the speaker was completely familiar, smooth and girlish, with just a trace of a British accent.

Catherine Hill had starred in so many movies over so many years that a Buddhist priest from Mars might be the only individual in the galaxy not to recognize it instantly.

"Hello, Miss Hill. My name is Madeline Bean. I have a gift to deliver."

"Yes?" she said sweetly. "From where?"

"My friend just bought Dickey McBride's home. We

years ago played the second Von Trapp daughter in *The Sound of Music,* or Snoop Doggy Dogg or the guy who does the voices on *Pinky and the Brain.* Without this greeting, most Hollywood insiders would be put momentarily ill at ease, and wonder how your mother raised you.

"I'm sorry I didn't call first to set up an appointment, but then I didn't have your phone number . . ."

"No, of course not. How could you? It's impossible to get my phone number. It's not only unlisted, it practically doesn't exist." Her dancing voice dipped and then returned in that pleasant musical way she had. I was mesmerized. The same charming voice that said, "I'll always love you, Frank, but I can never forgive you," on-screen to Gary Cooper, was now addressing me.

Catherine Hill smiled. "Finding my house, on the other hand, is never a problem. Just follow any tour bus up the street. They point this place out once every fifteen minutes without fail."

"Oh dear," I said with a trace of dismay in my voice, bonding a bit with the superstar movie queen of old over the sad lack of privacy one in her position must bear. Well, I mean . . . I could imagine it would be tough, couldn't I? I had empathy.

"Please, come in," she said sweetly. Throughout our little chitchat on the front steps, I knew she had been checking me out. What variety of stranger was I? A mental case who might cause injury? A rabid fan? A souvenir hunter who would dig up a plant or steal one of her little porcelain poodles? An Herbalife saleswoman?

I had dressed in my "good" clothes, ones that have labels people like Catherine Hill would recognize. Thanks to Wesley's mother I had a small supply of such outfits. Mrs. Westcott is a clotheshorse and just my size. For years she has sent me last season's wardrobe whether I could use it or not. To make a good impression on Catherine Hill, I wore a St. John knit suit in navy blue and white.

The star opened her front door wider to me. "Oh! Dear child. What have you brought me?"

My hands were full. I had carried from the car Dickey's

"Yes." Miss Catherine Hill gave me a rather penetrating look with her deep turquoise eyes. "I thought I recognized your name." She had known who I was all along. Of course. Fame was the game she played best.

At close range, Catherine Hill looked somewhat better and yet somewhat worse than she had in the bright outdoor light. Age could not be denied. Her famous sharp chin was now only sharpish, and set in a rounder face. The profile of her famous heart-shaped face was still strikingly heart-shaped, only now the silhouette was subtly softened with years. She must have been close to seventy-five, but she looked at least ten years younger than that. In her heyday, in the fifties and sixties, she was described as having the loveliest lips on the Silver Screen. Now, their strong shape owed much to the curvy outline that was penciled in. In all, her strong beauty was still evident, if paying its dues to time.

"Come into the little parlor," she said, cheerful as ever, leading the way. "Let's look at what you brought me."

Down the hall she turned to the left and we entered a chintz-covered den. The walls were padded and upholstered in an English print featuring big puffy pink hydrangea blooms amid green leaves. In fact, an entire English country garden bursting with flowers of all sorts covered each and every cushion and pad and sofa and window. I set the rose-wood case down upon a small black tole tray table, while settling my caterer's case in a corner beside a love seat.

I hadn't quite realized how petite Miss Hill would be. On the screen she had seemed tall and slim and in perfect proportion. In the bright chintz room, I realized she might only be five feet tall. And while her figure had filled out over the years, her hands and feet were quite small and dainty. She turned to me, and so naturally I stopped staring.

"Now this is from Dickey, did you say, darling?" She glinted her turquoise greens up at me.

"Yes. Would you like to hear a strange story?" I asked.

"My dear child, I live for it." She sat herself down in the center of one hydrangea-covered love seat and I took it for granted she wouldn't mind if I sat down as well. I chose a

Catherine Hill looked at me blankly. The name did not seem to register.

"Quita McBride . . ." I said, trying to make things clearer, and failing. ". . . um, I don't know her other name."

Catherine Hill did not seem to know her. "I assume this was the girl whom darling Dickey was schtupping at the time he died?"

I looked at her wide-eyed.

"You hadn't heard that rumor?" Catherine Hill looked extremely happy, just as I'd hoped. She loved to be the one to tell. "Frankly, I believe it. That's just the way Dickey would have liked to go out. I just don't remember if I ever met that last girl. They didn't have a big wedding. That I know. It must have been wedding number five or six for Dickey. I told him, after the fourth, just have something simple. That's what I did. Otherwise," she said, confiding in me, "it's just not in good taste."

I nodded. Heck, I should have been taking notes. These were the etiquette tips one so rarely finds in the pages of Emily Post.

"If there had been a wedding," Catherine Hill went on, "I'd have certainly been invited. It was our tradition, you see. We'd known each other for ages. Eons, actually. I like to say I'm the only beautiful woman in Hollywood that Dickey never slept with!" She laughed with glee, truly enjoying herself. I chuckled, too, careful to be polite.

"I attended four of Dickey's weddings and remember each one. Vivian Duncan planned some of them. Beautiful parties, beautiful. And of course I sent the rascal a disgustingly expensive gift for each one. I didn't mind, but it was always the girl who kept the gift. After a while, I simply had had enough. I mean, I still own every wedding gift Dickey ever bought for me."

I remembered that Catherine Hill had been married at least five times herself, and two of those husbands, she'd managed to marry twice. That's a lot of chatchkas.

"I told him. After that Emilette character took the lovely pair of sterling George II candelabras in the divorce settle-

"She taught him to play mah-jongg, and he came back to the set and taught me and the crew. We played every break. I couldn't even remember my lines half the time. Watch that film and see if I'm not stumbling all over the words. We were much too happy sitting around playing maj."

She smiled at the sweet memory of how truly difficult she once had been. I could only imagine some poor beleaguered director on a foreign location shoot with his prima donna of a leading lady refusing to come to the set because she wanted to finish her mah-jongg hand.

"The game is simply everywhere over there. They gamble in the streets. They gamble in those mah-jongg parlors, filled with smoke and Chinese men and drugs I wouldn't wonder. It can be very addictive. Do you play?"

I shook my head.

"Oh, you really should. It is too much fun. It really is."

"It's coming back into style," I said. "I'm trying to learn, but I don't have much time to play."

"Oh, I'll teach you. But don't bet big money, okay? Over the past forty years, I've lost more money to that old scalawag McBride. He was a cheat, I always said. But we couldn't catch him."

"He cheated at mah-jongg?" I had to laugh. It was hard enough for me to imagine this big-time movie star lothario playing mah-jongg with the girls, but cheating? That was funny.

"You know, dear one, your timing couldn't be better. All the maj girls are coming over in a few minutes. It's our old group—Dickey was a regular until a few years ago. They'll be tickled to find out that Dickey wanted us to have his old set of tiles."

"You're playing today?" I asked, sounding genuinely surprised. Hey, maybe I should consider acting. "So, you do recognize the set?"

"Oh, of course, sweetie." She pulled open the little drawers and opened the top of the box. "It was Dickey's pride and joy, this set. We always figured he used these tiles to put a hex on us. We could never win. But it's almost impossible to

Chapter 19

"**A**hem."

I jumped.

At the doorway to the chintz parlor stood a woman with steel gray hair clipped very short, just like a man's. She wore a gray pantsuit, which perfectly matched her hair. Her sharp jaw and slender nose reflected a sense of beauty past, and I figured the woman to be in her mid-sixties.

"Yoo-hoo?" She made it a question. "Where's Cath?"

I noticed her staring at my hand. I quickly pulled it back from the small, perfect Renoir. Her gaze moved down to the low tray table and rested on the antique mah-jongg chest.

"Holy Toledo. Is that Dickey's?" she asked.

"Rosalie, doll." Catherine Hill floated into the room in a swirl of green-silk fabric and a waft of Joy perfume. "Rosalie. Look what turned up on my doorstep."

She was talking about the mah-jongg set, not me.

"Yes, I saw."

Catherine Hill's lovely voice went quite deep with what sounded like sorrow. She patted the rosewood case lightly. "We miss you Dickey boy."

"And you have a visitor?" The woman looked at me with open curiosity.

Catherine cooed. "Madeline Beall, this is Rosalie Apple."

"Nice to meet you, Beall."

"It's Bean, actually. Madeline Bean. Nice to meet you."

"Bean?" Rosalie's face took on a pained expression. "Oh,

"What was she called, again?" Rosalie asked.

"Quita," Catherine answered.

"Quita McBride," Rosalie repeated. "Now that's a name."

"Actually, it's a very sad story," I said. "She fell the other night, and I'm afraid she died." I watched both women for reactions.

Catherine said. "In that accident? It was on the news."

I nodded.

"I hadn't heard that," Rosalie said, startled. "She was very young, wasn't she? I'm sure she was. Oh, dear."

Catherine continued as if Rosalie had never interrupted. "After they met, Dickey stopped coming to our games regularly. Remember that, Rosalie? When Dickey stopped bringing his antique Chinese set?"

"I never remember anything anymore," Rosalie said. She wore a pair of reading glasses on a golden chain around her neck and she pulled them up onto her nose and looked more closely at Dickey McBride's old mah-jongg case. "I have a terrible memory, you know that. It could have been five years or ten years, don't ask me."

"Well, that's rather interesting," I said. "My partner bought Mr. McBride's old house up on Wetherbee Drive. It turns out that this mah-jongg set was hidden behind one of the walls. It had been plastered up in an old fireplace."

"You're joking," Rosalie said.

"Fancy that," said Catherine Hill.

"But this is the part that gets really odd . . ."

Both women leaned forward. I wasn't sure it was because of the suspense of my story or just the fact that their hearing wasn't as good as it once was. I spoke up a little more clearly, just in case.

"Just the other day, a man came along from out of nowhere. He knocked me down and grabbed this mah-jongg set and ran."

"Oh, good heavens!" Rosalie said, clutching the front of her gray blazer.

"Terrible! The street crime these days. It's the homeless! No one does a thing about them." Catherine Hill shook her head sadly and turned to her old friend with an added com-

lacquered hair was a shade of bottle black that was startling against her pale wrinkled face. It looked like a hard-shell beehive with a tiny flip at the ends.

Amid the tumult and the laughter, the subject of Dickey McBride and the theft of the mah-jongg case had been dropped cold.

Instead, Catherine Hill began introductions once again. Everyone seemed eager to check out the new girl. It was a heady feeling. Inside this movie star's castle, clucked over by her movie-star friends, I'd suddenly become the center of attention.

"Girls! Girls! You must meet Madeline Beall."

My guardian angel can always be counted on to kick a little sand of reality into my starry eyes.

And no, I didn't correct Catherine Hill again. I didn't want to annoy her, frankly. She was too up. I was Catherine Hill's toy du jour, and she loved to see all the fuss I generated. As she introduced each woman, she reeled off an abbreviated bio of each.

Eva James, slender to the point where she might have proved useful to med students cramming for their skeletal anatomy exams, was, Catherine announced in mellifluous tones, ". . . an Oscar-winner for *Two on the Town*."

"I loved that movie," I piped up in a pretty gush.

This is required, as I'm sure you remember from the previous lecture. Needless to say, one neither needs to have loved the specified movie, nor even have seen it to gush thus. However, in the case of *Two on the Town*, I had and I did. This was one of the real kicks of meeting genuine Hollywood royalty. All the de riguer little niceties were startlingly sincere.

"That," Catherine continued, "was the first time Eva had costarred with Donald O'Connor and, we always tell her this—Eva stole the picture."

Rosalie picked up the tale. "Donald never forgave Eva and wouldn't costar with her again until Louie Mayer made him."

The four women giggled.

"Oh girls." Eva said, shushing them. But you could tell

he was gone." That theatrical trick of lowering her voice to a whisper was effective. I swear, I could be picking up dozens of acting tips if I was ever so inclined, just watching all these elderly divas peck at one another.

Eva James, blond and cool, looked at me with open curiosity. "Don't tell me this is Dickey's last wife. Not how I remembered her at all. Or had he gotten a newer one that I hadn't been aware of?" Her hand went to her throat and caressed a strand of pearls that were large enough to be gumballs.

Catherine Hill shouted above the clamor of the other ladies as they set to squabbling and correcting one another and chastising the new ones. "No, no. Now let's not go picking on poor Dickey again. He was my oldest friend. We started at MGM together when we were just kids. He was a charmer, which was why everyone loved him. He was gorgeous, too."

Hot dog. We were back to talking about McBride.

"Yes," Catherine continued, "he was a rake and a scoundrel, but he was also our friend. We played mah-jongg together for close to forty years. And no one here should throw stones."

"We always had fun gambling with Dickey," said Helen, the early TV star, "even if he did take my money. What do I care, ducks? I get residuals forever." She gave me a big wink with one false-eyelashed, elderly eye. "Eva never liked losing, though, did you?"

"Nonsense. Dickey was great fun." The tall, thin, blond former song-and-dance star shook her head, setting her drop diamond earrings to swinging. "Dickey and I were practically engaged at one time. I got a ring out of him, anyway."

"Enough chitchat," Rosalie said. "Let's play mah-jongg. The sooner we play, the sooner we eat, and I'm starving."

"Yes, me too," said Helen.

Rosalie eyed Catherine. "What is it going to be today, Cath? Deli?"

"Rosalie," Catherine said, playing the hurt hostess to nice effect, "You love deli. We always have deli. It's a tradition."

"It's cheap," Rosalie countered.

"Divine!" Catherine's manager, Rosalie Apple, stood up and clapped her hands in happiness.

I was encouraged and went on. "To start, a salad of hearts of romaine with roasted corn and avocado and a garlic-lime vinaigrette."

"Yum!" Eva James stood up on her long, if elderly, dancer's legs and joined the applause.

"Lovely," chimed in *Mike Heller*'s gal Friday, Helen Howerton, joining the others in an ovation to food, glorious, food.

And so, with such a ridiculously easy bribe, I was able to stay at the party. I only hoped I could string the courses out long enough to find out more about Dickey McBride and the book I felt was the root of so much that had yet to be explained. With enough good food, and enough time, I was determined to get one of these old movie queens to cough up a memory that would finally make sense of it all.

Catherine Hill's formal dining room with its lush view of the grounds in back.

While I had been busy in the kitchen, Catherine's maid, Sonia, had joined me. I considered Sonia my sister in crime, of course. Sonia had been the one who gave me the heads-up about the proper day and time I could expect to find the mah-jonggers at the house. And as I stir-fried the shredded duck and finished off the soup, Sonia stuck by my side in Catherine Hill's amazing kitchen. She insisted on helping, and I enjoyed her company. I had suggested she set the dining room table for four, not wanting to be too forward.

As soon as the group arrived in the dining room, they crowed and hooted and brayed in delight. Well, that's how it sounded to me, like a barnyard of elderly farm animals at feeding time. I was immensely pleased. I enjoy cooking, but I also enjoy getting a big reaction.

The savory aroma of the freshly prepared Wild Cherry Fettuccine was hard to resist.

"Look at this!"

"I need a refill on Tommy Collins!"

"How beautiful, Beall. It looks too pretty to eat!"

As they were getting settled in their seats at one end of the mammoth burl walnut dining table, I stepped forward.

"I prepared a West Indian Calabaza Soup," I said, and removed the lid of a splendid Royal Doulton soup tureen. Steam curled up.

"What is that, Beall?" Rosalie Apple had taken a strange liking to me, and it evidently had something to do with my new nickname.

"Please, sit down with us, Madeline," Catherine Hill said. "Sonia, bring a place setting for Madeline."

I sat down as instructed. "It's a fresh tomato-and-calamari soup."

"Ah."

"And there's a risotto cake that floats in it, you see." I served a bowlful to the hostess as her guests looked on greedily.

"Well, this sure beats the hell out of corned beef and

"Dickey couldn't write a to-do list, let alone a novel," Rosalie said.

The other women continued to eat, but paid careful attention to my story.

"The sad part is, Wesley and I actually found a book."

"You did?" Helen looked intrigued. I wondered if her old gal Friday role to *Mike Heller, Private Eye* was kicking in on a subconscious level.

"Yes. It was hidden in Dickey's old mah-jongg case. But, unfortunately we lost it. The mugger dropped the mah-jongg case but took that book."

"How mysterious," Eva said.

"That last evening I talked to Quita, she talked about you, Miss Hill, and your mah-jongg group, and she said that Dickey wanted you to have the set when we got it back from the police. That's why I brought it to you today. I was wondering if any of you know anything at all about that book?"

They looked at one another, but no one seemed to know anything.

I was finished here. I'd charmed and gushed. I'd wheedled and gossiped. I'd brought gifts and cooked, and then out-and-out begged. But I had nothing at all to show for it.

"I'm sorry, Madeline," Catherine Hill said, picking her fork up again. "We don't have the answers you are looking for. I hope you are not too disappointed."

"Thanks for listening," I said.

"You look so upset, my dear," Eva James said as she finished another Tom Collins.

"If you'll excuse me, I'll go get the dessert," I said.

"Dessert. How splendid!" Catherine beamed at her guests. "I knew we'd have fun today. My horoscope said so."

As they talked and teased each other, I went back through the butler's pantry, the little room which led to the large blue-and-white tiled kitchen. The sound of a lawn mower droned from outside. I peeked out between the white plantation shutters that covered the butler's pantry's one small window. In the intense afternoon sunlight, I could see the

"We all have secrets, Catherine. I'm sure there are things about you in Dickey's diary."

"Everyone has secrets. Dickey taught me that. Even her."

"Yes, we all put up the money. We should burn the book together."

"I can understand why you would want to burn it, Rosalie. Dickey wasn't a fool. He kept financial records, dear. And your bookkeeping was not . . ."

"Enough, Cath! She'll be back any minute. I wish she'd just leave us alone."

"What?" Catherine Hill sounded aghast. "Play your parts, my dears. I, for one, would be very disappointed to miss dessert."

On either side of the narrow butler's pantry, glass-front cabinets reached to the ceiling. They displayed enormous collections of fine china and crystal. As I waited silently in the small room, I began to feel suffocated by Catherine Hill's wealth and possessions. Eavesdropping made me feel anxious, sick, and nauseous. There was a pause in the conversation on the other side of the door, and then Catherine Hill's voice spoke up.

"Did you hear about Bella? Her daughter had another baby."

"No!" several voices responded.

The conversation had moved on. I had too many unanswered questions. What money had they all paid? And had these old women sent the gardener AKA chard man to steal that red book? They must have. I was unable to form one cogent thought.

"This is her fifth," Eva's voice was saying, "and that's just too many children . . ."

The women continued to prattle on about their friend's grandchildren, so I left my awkward lurking spot. Quickly, I walked across to the opposite door, the one that led into the kitchen, and shoved it open. Sonia looked up at me, startled. She was eating lunch while standing at the black-granite countertop.

"Oh, Miss Madeline," she said, smiling shyly. "This is delicious. Thank you for making a plate with the duck for me."

other. And then, the first name might not have been Jade, at all."

Now what was all this about? Was she just blowing smoke? I had enough to keep straight without being thrown off the scent by Eva James and her story of some old affair.

"You should ask Cath. She knew all about that affair. Cath was working with Dickey at the time. In the Orient, I think. Was that *East Meets West*? No, it was another one. The one where Cath sang. Oh, Lord, that was awful. God love her, they had to dub over every damn note. Marni Nixon did it. She did all of the singing in those days. But not for me, of course. Honey, God gave me a throat, and I sang like a bird."

I tried to get Eva back on track. "And that's when Dickey McBride was having a hot romance with a woman whose name might or might not have been Jade? Okay." Good try, Eva. I think not. I smiled pleasantly. "Well, thanks. That might help."

Sonia quietly returned with Eva James's fresh drink and set it down on the counter. Just then, Catherine Hill entered the kitchen, her famous face floating above that large turquoise muumuu. She looked concerned. "So here you are."

If food has power, dessert has the most. I was counting on it. I had a plan.

"It's time," I said, "for Tiramisu."

"Yes?" Catherine perked up immediately. "Oh, goody."

And then, into the kitchen walked an amazingly fragile old lady, the size of an elf. Her snow-white hair wisped down around her small head from a gold turban. She was dressed exactly like Catherine Hill, down to the gold ballet slippers and flowing turquoise shift.

"Is it time for dessert?" she asked.

"Mama? Are you up from your nap dear? Meet our new friend, Madeline. She's a very clever cook. She made the girls a marvelous lunch."

"Is that dessert?" the tiny old woman asked again.

How totally bizarre. Mother and daughter, dressed as twins.

room wasn't large, but it was pretty, decorated in a soft shade of peach and neatly kept. The heavy peach damask bedspread showed only the slight indentation made, I was sure, by the body of a napping woman who could only weigh eighty pounds.

Where would they hide the book? I pulled up the peach dust ruffle and checked under the bed, I tried opening a few dresser drawers. No dice. I walked across the small room and entered the adjoining bathroom. It, too, was decorated in the same shade of peach. The sink and the toilet and the tub, everything the same. The little room was perfectly clean. On the sink was a glass holding Mama's dentures.

Their secrets. Their secrets were submerged. What did that remind me of? It was a line. A line from a movie. It was a line in one of Catherine Hill's movies, but which one? I thought it out. I had rented a bunch of old films not long ago. Holly and I stayed up late watching them. Yes! *Heavenly Girls in the Forbidden City*. Teenaged Helen Howerton was hiding teenaged Catherine Hill's diary from the nuns. And where did she hide it?

The toilet. I picked up the heavy peach porcelain top and moved it slightly ajar.

Astounding. There, taped to the inside of the tank, submerged in cold water, was a large clear plastic storage bag, the kind famous for its airtight seal. Catherine Hill watched those commercials.

I pulled the bag out of the tank and dried it using one of Mama's fluffy peach terry-cloth bath towels. Inside the bag I could clearly see the prize.

With one quick unzip, I had my hands on Dickey McBride's red-leather book. I was high with my triumph. Here, too, in fact, was even the silver case that held the dragon dagger. I had lied, eavesdropped, and prowled, but I was victorious.

Unfortunately, I didn't have another second to enjoy the thrill of espionage. For at that moment, I heard a noise. I looked up. The knob on the door to the little peach bathroom was turning.

"Would you please?" I asked, finding a smile somewhere and pasting it on.

"Of course. Why, of course." Minimom doddered her way out, slowly, very slowly closing the door behind her.

In an instant, I readjusted the tank, flushed the toilet for verisimilitude, and stood straight up, checking to see that my short navy blue suit jacket would cover the back of my skirt where the bulky package was hidden. It would just have to do.

I pulled open the door. The old woman was about to leave her bedroom. No, no. I couldn't have her tell her daughter that she'd found me in her bathroom. Even if the poor old dear hadn't yet realized how physically close I had been to their hidden secrets, Catherine Hill would guess my motives in a half a second.

"Minnie," I said loudly, mindful of her hearing aid.

"Wha . . . ?" She stopped and slowly turned back. She saw me and smiled. "Take your time, young lady. Wash your hands. Do whatever you need to do. I will go—"

"No, no, no, no!" I rushed over to her and turned her around, faced her back toward her own little bathroom. "Your dentures . . . remember?"

"Oh." She looked startled, raising her hand to her sunken mouth. "Oh, yes. Thank you, dear." And without another thought, she headed back toward her bathroom.

I eased myself out the door of her room, back into the kitchen. How much time would little mama take to put in her choppers and get back to the gang? How long until she told of the terrible faux pas, walking in on a young lady in the john. I knew I didn't have much time to get out of there.

"Miss Madeline," Sonia called, catching sight of me.

"I'm in a hurry. Thanks for your help, Sonia." I grabbed my purse and moved across the kitchen, fast. I had to get to the front door before any of Catherine Hill's friends suspected I had found Dickey McBride's red book.

"You're leaving?" Sonia's voice trailed after me, but I was already down the main hall and almost into the entry. I pulled open the front door, glancing back inside the house, afraid someone would jump out and stop me.

now slipping down behind me at an alarmingly quick rate of speed. The good news: I had somehow luckily managed to stick the zipped package inside the waistband of my underwear as well as my skirt, and the damn bag wasn't likely to slip much further.

Unless . . .

I realized with a rising trill of panic, how gravity works. How heavy the package felt now that it was no longer wedged between my back and the tight waist of my suit skirt. What if the weight of the small red-leather book and the silver dagger case was stronger than the elastic that held up my damn panties? I had a momentary out-of-body awareness; the vivid flash of me, standing near the steps of Catherine Hill's mansion, threatened with a garden implement, with my silk underwear falling down around my ankles and the red book sitting on the pavement for chard man to find.

"Catherine and I made up," I said, talking faster. "She and I just had lunch. You've seen my car here, haven't you? We are just fine. But if I don't get the new *Soap Opera Digest* I promised her right away, I'm afraid she'll be cross with me. I must run this errand, and fast."

"You're getting her a magazine?" he asked, still upset. But I had gotten his attention. He earned his living making the grande dame inside the mansion happy.

"She said to be back in ten minutes and it's already been . . ." I looked at my watch, crossing my legs as subtly as I could. Hell. It had been ten minutes already. Minimom was probably right this very minute telling her upsetting tale about finding that young lady cook in her peach bathroom. I looked at the front door, sure it would open immediately, my panic real.

"She wants it right away?" he said, connecting the real fear on my face to the fear he must live with on a daily basis—of the consequences of not pleasing the boss lady.

"Could you just hit the gate button for me, and I'll run down to Sunset? I'll be back in a few minutes, and maybe Miss Hill won't be mad at me." Hey, we were on the same team, see?

He put his tool down and moved across to one of the front

Chapter 21

*B*ack at home, several hours later, I felt the need to be outside. The January night was mild and cool, probably mid-
fifties, but I was running a little hot. I needed to clear my
head after spending the last hours of the afternoon indoors
reading the red book.

In the little courtyard behind my house, a high retaining
wall was literally all that separated me from the Hollywood
Freeway. The city-built cinder-block wall was covered now
with sprays of bougainvillea vines and white twinkle lights.
A steady hum of unseen freeway traffic droned like a passing jet. I had become so accustomed to living with this
neighbor that I almost didn't notice the rush of noise as I en-
tertained a late-night guest. We had to sit close together,
Honnett and I, in order to hear each other clearly.

I had called Honnett to tell him the news. I needed to tell
him about the red book and what it meant. But our positions
were difficult, as always. He needed rules. I needed answers.
And there were other things that would be left unsaid.

"Maddie, don't do this to me. I'm a cop."

I looked up at Honnett. He was rubbing his eyebrows like
that would help ease us out of the trouble he was sure I'd
gotten into.

"Listen. It was all right, I think."

"Really?"

We were sitting in the cold on a patio bench. I think neither of us was ready to be alone together inside my warm

"Nice detail, Bean. Less graphic, please," he said, going back to rubbing his eyebrows.

"And the cool thing was, I made it out of there. It felt electrifying, you know? Like very powerful. I think I drove seventy-five all the way home."

"Don't tell me this, Mad. I'll worry about you. I mean it."

I smiled. "There I was, wasting my time all afternoon, chatting politely and flattering those old movie sweethearts, and cooking for them, and what did that get me?"

"I'm impressed. It got you inside the house."

"Yes. But I got nothing."

He put his arm around me, casually. I liked it there just fine. I think he was figuring he might as well accept what I'd done.

"It wasn't until I starting working smarter, not harder, that I found out anything at all."

"Please, Maddie. Don't give me all the details, okay? Seriously."

"Okay. But Wesley and I read McBride's diary. It was all handwritten, which was not so easy to read. There were plenty of references that were so obscure we couldn't figure them out. Lots of dates and initials. But we marked two passages that could be important."

"So what do you think happened?" Honnett asked. "Are you saying these old movie stars were behind the mugging in Santa Monica?"

"Of course they were. Aren't you paying attention here? I saw the freaking chard guy riding the freaking power mower over Cath Hill's freaking Marathon II sod! It was him. He was even wearing the gold ring I remembered. And then later . . ." I stopped. After all, didn't Honnett just say he couldn't handle all the details? I tried a different tack.

"Let me try to explain. After Wes found the mah-jongg set hidden behind the wall at Wetherbee, the only person he called was Quita McBride. He told her he was busy all day, meeting me in the morning in Santa Monica, yadda yadda, working on the house. He offered to bring the maj set to her at the Sweet and Sour Club party that night. Wes was being

bee house, she didn't care that Wes and I had lost the mah-jongg case. She only wanted to hear about the red book. And she panicked when she realized it was gone. She had been counting on a big payoff from Catherine Hill. Without the book, she couldn't come up with the cash, and that scared her."

"Yes. I see that."

"It all fits. Those old women were scared of the book. When I was hiding in the pantry, I heard them talking, Honnett. I'm sure I'm right about this."

"Don't keep telling me about your illegal activities, Maddie. If you care for me at all."

I looked at him. The first personal comment of the evening. "Honnett, come on. I checked it all out with Paul. You remember Paul?"

"That lawyer you hang out with." He did not sound terribly impressed.

"Paul is the best lawyer on the planet. And he specializes in alternative law—you know, how to slip through the cracks and not get caught."

"A fine friend. Everyone should have one like Paul."

"Paul told me I don't have anything to worry about. First, I was invited into Catherine Hill's house as a guest. I didn't break in."

"Yes. Good."

"Second, I was preparing lunch with Catherine Hill's permission. No law against a caterer doing that. Believe me. And there's no law that Paul is aware of that prohibits a caterer from spending a little time in the butler's pantry."

"True."

"And third, I don't believe there are any laws against using the bathroom when you've been invited into someone's home."

"Yeah, okay."

"I didn't crack open any safes. I didn't pry open any locks. I simply took a little peek into the toilet tank . . ."

Honnett raised one eyebrow. It looked good on him.

". . . to make sure the ballcock was in operating condition . . . because . . ."

month, there was another mention of Rose. "Studio agrees to audit. Rose is raging mad." And another entry, three months later. "Showed Rose ledger. Embezz?"

Honnett looked at me. "Who's Rose, then?"

"Well, today I met Rosalie Apple. She had been McBride's manager at one time, and he fired her. This was all a long time ago. I'm guessing Rose was his nickname for Rosalie. I'll have to check on the dates and things. I'm guessing there were irregularities with royalty payments. As McBride's manager, Rosalie Apple got all his checks. Perhaps she kept more than her ten percent."

"This was years ago. McBride never pressed charges. Do you expect me to go after some old lady without any evidence?"

"Do you always have to ruin my buzz, Honnett? No one is asking you to arrest anyone. Jeesh."

He smiled at me, trying to relax a little. "It's hard enough for two people to get together without all of their personal garbage getting in the way, you know? On top of that, you go dragging all sorts of professional crap into the mix."

"Calm down, Bubba," I said, and gave him a peck on the cheek. "We'll be fine. We will. Just don't come busting down so hard on my good day's work."

He took my hand. "Sorry about that."

My goodness. The man said he was sorry, and it hadn't killed him. I was beginning to have hope.

"You said there were two things in that red book you got excited about. What was the second one?"

"Well, back at the house today, Eva James told me some odd story about a girl named Jade. She told me Dickey had an affair with this Jade back on a movie location in China. At the time, I was sure she was just trying to lead me off the track. But then, when Wes and I were reading Dickey's diary, we found some passages about Jade."

I filled Honnett in. The dates were back in 1947. They were datelined "Hong Kong." Dickey talked about Jade teaching him mah-jongg. He posted his winnings, taking quite a bit of cash off that film crew over the six months they were shooting *Flower of Love*. One entry read: "Jade my

prefers things light and romantic. I had definitely been thrown off my game. It was probably too late, now, to reverse the damage.

"So . . . you're tired of hearing about movie stars and their love affairs? Man, the *National Enquirer* would go broke if everyone were like you."

"And," Honnett said, grinning, "that would be a bad thing?"

"So, are we still going to see that movie we talked about?" I asked.

"Sure," he said. "Why don't you call me when you have some free time."

I put my arms around his waist and pulled him toward me. Leaning forward, going up on my toes to reach him, I gave him a slow kiss. I knew Honnett and I were not going to have a chance at any sort of real relationship until I got this whole Quita McBride thing out of my system. I just wanted to mark my place. I just wanted him to still want me when it was all over.

ley at the Farmer's Market, but figuring that out and finding the red book had brought me no closer to understanding what had happened to Quita McBride.

I found my black clogs and stepped into them.

Those old movie stars. They took a stupid risk. I had read McBride's diary with Wesley, and then again later last night. There was simply nothing in it that was worthy of theft, much less murder. The tepid long-ago scandals that were mentioned would hardly shock anyone today. Dickey's diary was from the forties, with a marked forties-era sensibility. It hinted darkly at infidelities of the day. It noted rumors of certain celebrities' closeted homosexuality, and detailed petty studio betrayals, all among figures whose glory days were half a century ago, and most of whom had now been dead for years. In today's culture, most of these scandals would be thought of as staggeringly boring.

I shook my head. Only the puffy egos of women like Catherine Hill and Eva James and Helen Howerton could lead them to imagine that their old secrets were news. All that fuss and all that bother and nobody cared anymore what they did.

But there was something else that was not quite right. Even with all these answers, I now began to realize I hadn't been asking the right questions. Catherine Hill might have sent someone to grab the book, but she wouldn't have harmed Quita. Once Catherine got her hands on McBride's diary, Quita would no longer have been a threat. After all, Quita hadn't even seen the book yet.

I roamed around downstairs in the kitchen, putting on the teakettle, getting a big white mug, rooting around for some soothing carbohydrates to nibble with my tea as I thought it all over.

Had Quita's death been an accident? Then why had she seemed so terrified when we saw her? Why had she begged me for help? What had she been afraid of? It still didn't add up.

The pine farm table near the back of my kitchen had ten chairs around it, but I picked my usual spot at the end.

I had to start over. Eliminate the mystery of that damn

Heights was much quieter than mine. Birds perched on an overhead wire sang sweetly, oblivious to the recent calamity.

I rang Buster Dubin's doorbell and waited.

To my surprise, Trey answered the door. "Hey. Madeline. What's up? You looking for Bus?"

"Yes. Is he home?"

"Sure, come on in," he said. "We're sitting out back, drinking Bloody Marys. We have a pitcher."

I stepped in and was greeted by Buster's gold-leaf Buddha, smiling benevolently from his place of honor in the entry. The fellow seemed to be the only one who was sanguine enough in the face of such disturbing events to hang on to his grin.

I followed Trey through the darkened house.

"I thought you were traveling out of town this week," I said, just making conversation. I remembered Trey was a sales rep with manufacturing accounts in Indonesia and the Far East.

"Right. Well we're *not supposed to leave*," he said, whispering the last part in mock menace. He sounded rueful. "They scared us shitless, the cops. They were pretty uncool."

Ah. Honnett had been there. I hoped Buster wouldn't hold it against me. At least he hadn't been arrested.

Trey walked through his friend's house barefoot. He wore a rumpled black T-shirt with the sleeves cut off and a pair of drawstring pants. As we stepped outside into the dappled sunlight, I noticed Trey's normally tawny skin had a slightly grayish cast.

Buster looked up from reading the paper. "Maddie? Hey." He jumped up and kissed my cheek and then pulled over a third oversize teak patio chair to the table. "How cool is this?"

Trey poured himself another Bloody Mary and offered one to me.

"No, thanks. I'm just here for a minute."

"I'm glad you stopped by," Buster said. "I've been meaning to call you. We're going to cancel the Sweet and Sour Club for a while."

"So," I said to the guys. "I hear they're keeping you both close to home still. The police. I'm sorry it's been so harsh."

"I am over that, Madeline," Buster said. His grin reminded me of the Buddha statue in his front hall. "You know how it goes in this devilish world. You cannot escape your karma."

Trey snorted. "Right, man."

Buster ignored Trey and continued, "I figure that it is not my karma to be directing that *Warp* music video in Copenhagen. I'm cool with that. I figure there must be a higher plan. You dig?"

Actually, I did.

Buster said, "But my man Trey here is freaking."

I looked at Trey. He certainly looked bad.

"I need to get to China, brother," Trey said. "I got business, you understand? These Chinese partners don't get why I'm not over there right now. It's so stupid."

"You know what would make you feel better?" Buster asked his friend.

I quickly thought of several good answers: sleep, a change of clothes, something to consume that didn't include alcohol as its main ingredient . . .

"You should jump in the pool," Buster said. "It will cool you off, bro."

Trey drained the ice-cube melt from the bottom of his glass and stood up. "I think I will. You coming?"

"In a minute," Buster said. "Go ahead. You gotta chill."

Trey left us and walked down to the large swimming pool way down at the end of the property. I watched him in the distance as he pulled off his shirt and stripped down to his boxers. Athletic and slim, Trey Forsythe dived off the side into the pool, sending perfect aqua ripples up onto the glassy surface.

"He's been so out of it," Buster said. And then he leaned over and opened a cooler, bringing out two bottles of Arrowhead water. He set one frosty bottle before me and then unscrewed the cap of the other one for himself.

"Thanks," I said. "What's wrong with Trey? Is he staying here?"

"Quita was very upset about money, too, wasn't she? But didn't she inherit a bundle when Dickey McBride died last year?"

"Well, you would have thought so, wouldn't you? But there are still some legal things that were up in the air. These lawyers are bloodthirsty mothers. You know. And they thought Quita was dim. They were dragging her over coals. Red-hot coals."

"About what?" I asked.

"There are always technicalities. Paperwork, whatever. Quita was always tense about it."

"Buster, did Quita ask you for any money lately?"

He nodded, matter-of-fact. "Everyone is always asking Buster for money."

"That's what has been puzzling me. I barely knew Quita, and she asked me for money, too. Why? Did Quita tell you what she needed the cash for?"

"Maybe lawyers? I don't know. Verushka came up to me at the Sweet and Sour Club and asked for twenty grand, too."

"Really?"

"Yeah, she told me it was to pay off a loan or something."

"And Trey?"

"He said he was in trouble with some guys."

"So will you lend it to him?" I asked.

"He's a big boy. He'll go to work and sell another hundred containers of bicycle parts or whatever shit he sells," he said, referring to Trey's commissions from his import sales gig.

"You think?"

"It's a tough world out there, Mad. It'll all be okay. Don't you worry. Somehow, people cope."

Do they? I wondered. Did Quita "cope"?

"Say," I said, changing the subject. "Do you know if Verushka's working today?"

"She works every day. You want her address?" He pulled a pen from his pocket, and I gave him a notepad from my purse.

"You seem calmer than the last time I saw you, Buster."

Chapter 23

In September of 1917, Harry Culver incorporated his own city, just east of the beach resort known as Venice, California. He was quite a promoter. He bussed people into his new burg and gave them a "free lunch." He offered free land to the winner of the prettiest baby contest. He started a marathon car race. But his biggest marketing brainstorm was so effective it forever altered the history of Culver City. He enticed early movie man Thomas Ince to relocate his Sunset Boulevard studio facilities to 10202 Washington Boulevard. In 1924, a roaring lion moved in. Metro-Goldwyn-Mayer took over the forty-acre Goldwyn Studios. And Culver City became one of the major centers of this new screenland industry.

Even now, bought out with Japanese money and bearing a Japanese name, the same venerable old studio still stands. It was to this older Culver City neighborhood that I was headed. In the shadow of what is now called Sony Pictures Entertainment, on a side street off of Washington, was an old warehouse that housed the miniature-model shop of Mars/Kirschner Industries. I pulled up and easily found a spot to park on the street, a sure sign it was Saturday if there ever was one.

The plain-front gray building gave no indication of the work done inside. You couldn't tell from the exterior of the three-story-high structure what went on inside, and that's the way these businesses liked it. The warehouse fit into its nonde-

on a three-foot-high, twenty-five-foot-long replica of the Golden Gate Bridge, perfect down to the minute signs of oxidation on its rust-colored paint.

"We're going to blow that one up," Verushka said, walking up beside me. "Kaboom. I'm really excited about that."

I turned and said hello.

"These days," Verushka explained, "most movie effects are CG—you know, computer-generated. It's much cheaper, but we say, you get what you pay for. We're winning them back. Sometimes the effect is worth the time and money. You know they used miniature pistons in the engine-room scenes in *Titanic*."

"This is fantastic," I said.

"Thanks." Verushka turned to me. "What brought you down here? I was shocked to see you standing by the door."

"Hope I didn't scare you," I said.

"No, but technically, as far as our top-secret clients know, we are a secure site."

"Sorry, I forced my way in with gunfire and then tied up your receptionist."

Verushka laughed. "We have Dreamworks coming in today. If anyone asks, you're consulting on a kitchen environment for one of our space modules."

"Perfect," I said, smiling. "You know, Wesley would actually be great at that."

"Really? I should call him. So what's up?"

"Buster gave me your address. Can you spare a minute for a couple of questions?"

"Party questions? Come on out to my office," she said, giving me a big smile.

Verushka led me out of the workshop and back down the corridor. We soon stopped and she used a key-card to open a chartreuse green door. Her office was large and spotlessly white. There was a nice white-leather sofa in one corner, and she flopped down. She was dressed in casual clothes, a denim work shirt that she wore as a jacket over a T-shirt and pair of baggy shorts. It revealed a bit more of Verushka's thighs than I'd seen at the Sweet and Sour Club parties, and there was a bit more of Verushka to see in the daylight. Her

"What do you want me to say?" Verushka asked, her voice going up, her eyes opening wide. "I'm mortgaged up to my eyeballs here. My credit cards are maxxed. I just need a little cash flow."

I heard the same pitch of panic in Verushka's voice that I'd heard in Quita McBride's.

"Is it for someone else? Maybe for someone close to you?"

Her deep brown eyes didn't blink. Slowly she nodded.

"Who?"

"My boyfriend. You don't know him," she added. "He needs my help."

"I had no idea." This was an understatement. Verushka had always seemed like the lone strong woman type. And the guys with whom she played mah-jongg never talked about her boyfriend that I could remember. It just went to show that one really never knows. We don't always have time to pay attention. People are a mystery. "I didn't realize . . ." I said.

"I know," she said, sighing. "I've been pretty low profile about our engagement. That's the way he wants it. There are reasons." Verushka folded her plump hands in her lap.

Oh, man. What kind of guy encourages his "fiancée" to keep their relationship a big secret? Easy odds answer: a married one. Poor Verushka. I never understood women like Verushka, who allowed themselves to get involved with unavailable men. Or did I? I thought about Arlo for the first time that day.

But I felt sorry for her instantly. And on top of all that, he had money troubles.

I looked at Verushka and reassessed. In the time I'd known her, she'd impressed me as funny and outspoken and large and endearing. She reminded me of Velma on *Scooby-Doo*—quick and sincere, everyone's best friend. Only now I was beginning to worry that Velma had fallen for a bad dog.

"Why does your boyfriend need the money?"

"He's got debts. He's gotten behind in paying them off. I have to help him, Maddie."

"I see."

back? I'll put up my stock in this company as collateral. Please."

"Verushka." I looked at her. I knew she didn't want to hear what I had to say. That didn't stop me. "This guy sounds like big trouble. Do you really need this?"

"Do you believe in fate, Maddie? I do. Some things are beyond our power. And even though we might be in pain, we can't always control our own destinies. Some people have money problems. Perhaps that is my fiancé's fate. And it's my fate to love him."

Throw fate in my face? This is exactly why I have hated the concept all these years, hated the excuse it provides to people who don't want to take responsibility for solving their own problems, fixing their lives, growing up and healing themselves.

"Won't you help us, Maddie? Can't you find a way in your heart to give us a loan?"

Another woman in need, begging for my help. I felt the weight of it. Just the other night, I had turned Quita down, and now I was paying that price.

"You believe in fate, don't you?" Verushka asked.

"Well," I said, "right now, I don't believe I'm fated to lose twenty grand."

"Oh." Her dark brown eyes widened, clearly showing her pain. "I had such hope."

I had hopes, too. I hoped to find out what had happened that night to Quita McBride. We don't always get exactly what we hope for.

And then it all sort of just clicked together. Verushka was in love with a man who needed twenty thousand dollars to pay off gambling debts. Verushka had to keep her lover's name a secret. Quita McBride was also desperate to get her hands on a lot of money. Now what was the possibility that they were both trying to save the same man? And I thought, could it be Buster who is the man in need? Was Buster broke and stringing Verushka along? Is that why Buster couldn't lend money to his friends?

"Verushka, it's very important for me to know your boyfriend's name."

Chapter 24

"Hey, Madeline?" Buster opened the front door. "You forget something?"

"Yeah, I guess you could say that. I forgot to talk to Trey. Is he still here?"

"Trey? I think he's sleeping. He was on the patio a while ago."

"Would you mind if I checked?"

"Oh, sure. Come in. Yeah." Buster opened the door wider.

"Trey and you go back pretty far, right?" I walked in and stood in the entry, back once again in the presence of the golden Buddha.

"Since fifth grade. Long time." Buster walked me through the big house. He was now wearing his lucky red-silk jacket with the embroidered slogan *The Hand from Hell*. I figured he was playing mah-jongg on the computer before I interrupted. "It always amazes me," he said. "He doesn't go after chicks, they come after him." Buster turned and gave me a very deliberate look.

"Well, don't worry about me," I said, startled to the point of laughter. "I'm not interested in Trey."

"Good thing," Buster said. "I love the guy, Maddie. But he is not the easiest guy to love."

Buster opened the French door out to the patio for me. "Looks like he's still sleeping. But go on over. Maybe for you he'll wake up."

I crossed the flagstone patio. The teak table and chairs

"You could do worse."

My back was to the setting sun, and Trey squinted up at me.

"I don't think you want to get into event-planning, Trey," I said, finding a seat on the chaise next to him. "I just think you are looking for a way to raise some cash."

"What makes you think that?"

"Quita McBride."

"Now, I'm not following you at all . . ."

"Let's say Quita wanted to help you out. What would Quita do to raise money fast? She didn't have anything worth selling. But then she was reminded that her husband had kept a journal that might prove valuable. She hadn't paid much attention to the journal when Dickey was alive, but now that she was hungry to get cash, it probably sounded like her only shot."

Trey looked bored.

"Of course, Dickey's old diary couldn't do Quita any good as long as it was missing. But that all changed when Wes called. He'd found the old mah-jongg case hidden behind a wall. Quita was sure the diary had been kept in that case, but she couldn't wait to turn it into cash. So she called Dickey's old movie-star friends and offered to sell them the diary, sight unseen."

"You making all this stuff up?"

"But poor Quita didn't figure on just how badly those old ladies would want to protect their secrets. When they learned that Quita hadn't even seen the book yet, Catherine Hill and the others arranged to get the book back themselves. Faster and cleaner. The way they did it, Quita never got a chance to read any of their silly old secrets."

"Really?" Trey looked at me. "They sound pretty sharp."

"Sure." I took off my sunglasses, as the sun had begun to set. "So Quita was frantic, wasn't she? Wes and I saw her Wednesday evening. When she learned Dickey's mah-jongg case had been stolen and the red book was missing, she panicked. There was nothing to sell to the mah-jongg ladies. No more big payoff."

"So what did she do?" I asked.

"Come on, sit closer and I'll tell you," he said. "Quita sold that old house as fast as she could. But after paying off the mortgage and taxes and a whole load of other stuff, she didn't end up with much."

"And you grabbed whatever money she had, I'll bet. To pay off your debts."

"Don't look at me like I took it from her. She wanted to give it to me. It was her choice."

But what Trey was telling me didn't entirely scan with the fear I had seen in Quita McBride's eyes.

"Why don't you tell me the rest of it, Trey? Why she was frantic to raise money for you on Wednesday? It wasn't your fantastic body alone, was it? That's been over for months, right? Why don't you tell me what had Quita so motivated to help you out?"

"Why should I?"

I got up on one knee and moved to lean down over him as he reclined in the chaise. He looked up at me, surprised.

"Because," I said, my anger hard to contain, "I want to know." Then, to make him jump, I slammed my hand down on the side of the chaise lounge just a few inches from his ear.

But he didn't flinch at all. His face was now close to mine. I could feel his breath on my cheek. He reached up and took my other hand and placed it on the warm skin on the flat of his stomach.

"How badly?" he whispered. "How badly do you want to know?"

I left my hand where he'd placed it, not flinching myself. "What did you have on Quita? Something scared her. Was it your old affair? How could that . . . ?" I was lost. How could that be a threat? McBride was already dead.

But then, maybe we had all heard the story backward. My expression must have changed.

"Did you figure it out?" Trey reached up and slowly pulled on the clip that held my long hair back off of my face. A tumble of heavy hair fell forward.

The rumor had been slightly off.

out of the blue he says, 'no more.' No more. He's got a ton of it. He makes more off of directing one of those car commercials than I make in a year busting my hump arranging manufacturing deals in China. He could have solved the whole problem if he'd just agreed to give me another loan. But he wouldn't. Don't go feeling sorry for Buster. It's his own damn fault."

To support his gambling habit, good-looking Trey had used them all. First Buster, who had paid his friend's debts for years, then Verushka, who picked the wrong guy to love, and then there was Quita, whose fears about Dickey's death made her open to blackmail.

Trey watched me stand up. "You sure you want to leave?"

"I've heard enough. Unless you'd like to tell me about the night Quita died."

"What? What are you talking about?" For the first time, Trey sounded annoyed.

"Quita told me she was supposed to meet you after the party." She hadn't said anything at all about Trey, actually.

"Okay, sure. But I never came back to the house. What was the point? She hadn't gotten the money."

So, Quita had been expecting him that night. And how was I to know he really stood her up?

"Look." He sat up and made eye contact. "Lend me some money, Madeline. I know Buster. He'll get all concerned about you. He'll be raging at me. Then Buster will pay you back. You lose nothing."

"And why, Trey, would I ever do that?"

"You were looking at it when you first came outside. You know you want it."

"Oh," I said. Oh, *really*. "You're scaring me, Trey. You know me so well."

He smiled.

On some, sarcasm is entirely wasted.

"Madeline, you are really funny. Don't you remember that fortune cookie you e-mailed me the other night? It said, 'Taste everything at least once.' Follow your own damn advice, sugar. Come on down here. Take a taste."

I kept a tight rein on my rising disgust. Years of working

Chapter 25

*B*ellagio Road was quiet and dark as I pulled up in front of Catherine Hill's Bel Air estate. The gate was open this time, permitting access to the long driveway that was lined with old-fashioned lampposts. I followed the evenly spaced puddles of soft white light on the cobblestones all the way up to the house. Lit up at night, the home's formal pillars and classical façade gave it the look of a mausoleum. The entire scene seemed more imposing than I remembered it from yesterday's bright afternoon visit.

I noticed a couple of cars were already parked near the entrance. A Lincoln Town Car and an older Jaguar. I left my own Grand Wagoneer among them and took the steps up to the front door.

Before I could ring, the door was opened. Standing there was Catherine Hill.

"You are on time," she said, her voice pleasant, her light English accent charming as always. "Please come in."

Catherine was dressed in a long silver lounging robe, with a zipper up the front. And if silver lamé was not enough to make her fashion statement, there were white marabou feathers at the neckline and at the borders of each flowing sleeve. Tonight she had abandoned her turban and instead sported a highly piled platinum blond hairdo complete with perky bangs. It was a wig.

"Don't you look adorable," she said, ushering me inside, showing her famous dimple.

alie was dressed in a white oxford shirt with navy slacks and Gucci loafers, conservative as before.

Eva James looked up at me from the spot where she was seated, next to the fireplace. The fire's glow softened her tight jawline and lit up her sleek blond bob. In this light, she looked almost exactly as I remembered her in her glory days as queen of the MGM musicals. I suspected she always devised a way to sit near the edge of a lighted fire.

Helen Howerton and her zebras settled down on one of the three massive sofas that formed a U around the fireplace. Catherine and Rosalie took seats on the opposite sofa, and I decided to face the fire, on a sofa of my own.

I set the red-leather book down on my lap.

"Shall we chitchat, dear?" Catherine asked. "Or would you prefer to get down to business?"

She seemed calm and friendly. I suspected my recent theft of the red book had not pleased her one bit, but her talent to hide her true feelings was a gift, one I had witnessed before, in fact, the previous afternoon. We seemed to understand each other. We had both been deceptive. We had both discovered the other's deception. We were, therefore, very much alike. No need to make a scene. And besides, I had the red book and was about to return it. They dared not upset me now. Power, while fleeting, feels supremely cool.

"Could you please tell me what went on between you and Quita McBride?" I asked.

"All right," Catherine said, sounding perfectly agreeable. "She called me on Wednesday morning and told me she wanted to trade something valuable. She claimed that an old mah-jongg set had just been found. She reminded me that Dickey kept a diary and that there were many secrets in it that we girls wouldn't care to have come to the press. She said when the mah-jongg set was returned to her, she'd have the diary as well."

"She was attempting to blackmail you," I said.

"Filthy girl," Eva James said.

"She's gone now, dear," Catherine Hill said sweetly to Eva, then resumed her story. "Quita asked me to pay her

but they kept wandering off to check on all those zebras balancing on her big shirt.

Helen took up the story. "Flax said your partner, Wesley, was a very nice safe driver and so it was incredibly easy to follow him into Santa Monica. Flax had hoped the young man would leave the mah-jongg set in his parked car. That would have been easy. A quick little bash and bingo, another car theft in Santa Monica, and we'd have our diary. But no. Your partner took his bulky backpack along, so Flax simply had to follow."

"Your friend is very tall, Beall," Rosalie said. "Insanely easy to follow a tall man. Flax had no problem keeping him in sight, even walking around in that crowded outdoor market."

So, it was as simple as that. It was almost just after Wes arrived at the Market that we met up and he showed me the mah-jongg set. And soon after, this man Flax ran off with it.

"But this guy, Flax, he threw the mah-jongg set away," I said. "Why?"

"We didn't care anything about that old set of tiles," Helen Howerton said. "It was the diary we needed to get hold of. Hell, if Flax had been stopped and he was still holding on to that old wooden case, he'd be arrested. And then where would we be? His family has worked for Catherine forever. They'd track it back to us."

Catherine said, "I told Flax, go get the diary and whatever you do, ditch the old case. And he did what I instructed. He always does. Good man."

It wasn't that complicated, I realized. Wes and I had just stumbled into an old storyline that had been set in motion for decades. It seemed straightforward enough. And why, really, shouldn't these old ladies have their secrets back?

"You never gave Quita the money?" I asked.

"Of course not," Catherine Hill said, her voice for once sounding heated. "We got the diary, hadn't we? Why should we pay the silly thing a cent? But that wasn't as important to the girl as my testimony. She had really been quite desperate for me to stay mum."

out all the dates, but Dickey implied in his diary that Eva was married at the time to one of McBride's movie-star friends. Since Eva's last husband, an old Hollywood hoofer, was now dead twenty years, I wondered why she would care so much about the diary. But shame never died.

Helen Howerton, who played the teenaged sidekick to Catherine Hill in all those schoolgirl pictures, was another of Dickey's dates—five stars. I wondered if Dickey had to peel Helen out of her trademark loud prints when they tumbled into bed.

His book betrayed even Catherine Hill, the woman who claimed to be the one person in Hollywood with whom Dickey had never slept. McBride wrote that he'd been Catherine's very first lover, back in a dressing room when they were both in their teens, in the days when they played brother and sister in the movie *Summer Storms*.

"None of us has read the diary, you see," Rosalie said. "We couldn't."

"Then we'd see what he wrote about each other. That wouldn't do at all," Eva James said, looking eternally young next to the fireplace.

"Mama took care of it for us," Catherine Hill explained. "We gave it to Mama to keep nice and safe."

"We were going to burn it," Helen said.

"Yes, but we planned to do it all together," Catherine said. "Mama hid it for us, using the same trick that Helen and I used to hide a diary in our old *Heavenly Girls* movie." She eyed me. "But yesterday, when we realized you'd actually found our book—"

"We were shocked, you know," Helen said, interrupting.

"And amazed," added Eva James. "We thought we had been so clever. We were certain we had fooled you."

"Yesterday," Catherine repeated in a louder tone, taking back the stage, "when we realized that you found the book—why I swore up and down—"

"She did, too," Helen said.

"—and for the first time in my life," Catherine Hill continued, "well, I never thought I'd say this, Madeline, but I wished the Lord had made just one less Catherine Hill fan."

"Cath?" a small, reedy voice called out. Catherine Hill's little mama came teetering into the room. She was dressed, as I had now come to expect, head to toe in a duplicate copy of her daughter's silver lamé housecoat outfit. The marabou feathers came up so high on her neckline that they reached her small chin. There are no words to describe the wig.

"We're right in here, minimom!" Catherine called to her.

By the smile on the lips of the ninety-year-old Hill matriarch, I suspected she had once again forgotten her teeth in a glass.

"Are we having a party?" Mama Hill asked.

"Yes, Mama," Catherine Hill said, her voice sounding positively festive.

And then she took the red-leather book out of my hand and flung it directly into the center of the fireplace.

the midst of warbling, ". . . my Lost Lotus Flow . . ." went suddenly silent.

"First off," Wesley said, "Chinese is not one language, it's more like a language family. Think of Mandarin, Wu, Min, Kejia, Yue, Huizhou, Xiang and Gan, to give them their Mandarin names. Kejia is also known as Hakka, Min is also called Hokkien, and Yue is commonly known as Cantonese."

"Whoa," she said.

I peeked around and made eye contact with Holly. "You did ask."

"Well, I just thought the name of Catherine Hill's character sounded too cutesy. Tip Tang, whazzat?"

Wesley, on a roll, took on that question. "Transcription of Chinese into Latin letters has been a very tricky issue. Chinese languages have sounds that don't have easy equivalents in European languages. Also, Chinese languages are all tone-based, and how do you write that? Over the years, we've written their words using different phonetic spellings, but none of them sound exactly right."

"It confuses me," Holly said. "It seems like all the words have changed, too. Like do we still call it Peking Duck if the city is called Beijing now?"

Wes grabbed the popcorn bowl and helped himself. "We probably should. Most of the world has adopted a system of transliteration called Hanyu Pinyin, which is the official system of the People's Republic of China. That's why we now see words like Beijing, and Daoism and Mao Zedong."

"Hey, I want to watch the movie." I grabbed the remote from Holly when she wasn't paying strict attention and unmuted *Flower of Love*.

"I don't think I ever saw this one," Holly said, shifting her focus back to the screen. "It's pretty funky."

"I vaguely remember it," Wes said, "but I didn't remember how good old Dickey McBride was. He had a great voice."

The scene shifted to a palace garden, and we all made comments on the silk costume Catherine Hill wore.

"I can't believe how thin Catherine Hill was," I said. "And pretty."

Millie. Such a small item as the chill factor of hands could make or break you in Hollywood. Another mystery solved.

I gently reached over and plucked the remote out of Wesley's grip, intent on rewinding to the point earlier in the movie at which we had stopped.

"Wait," Holly commanded.

I paused the tape.

"Go in slow motion, Mad. Maybe we'll see someone listed in the credits named *Jade*."

Well. Duh.

The three of us stared at the tiny names as they crawled slowly up and off the TV screen. Many of the names of the crew and bit players were Chinese.

"No," Holly said. "No one named Jade."

"Hey, go through them again," Wes said, getting excited. "The Mandarin word for Jade is Ling. Look for Ling."

We were instantly alert. I quickly rewound the tape. Holly, on the left, sat cross-legged on the bed, rubbing her eyes. I rewound a bit too far. Wesley, in the middle, sat with a hand absently over his mouth in concentration. I hit play, and the terrible closing song began. I, sitting on the right, held my ears until we came to the names. I hit the slow-motion button and we stared again at the credit crawl.

"There." I stopped the tape. "That's not Ling, but it's close. What does that name mean, Wes?"

"Chen Liling," he read. "The name Chen is one of the most common Chinese surnames, and the two first names are Li and Ling, which mean 'beautiful jade.'"

Beautiful   Jade. . . . *met   Beautiful   Jade   for   the weekend . . .*

"That's it! That's it!" Holly crowed.

"Liling was an actress," I said, reading her small screen credit, wedged between dozens of Asian named bit players. I quickly rewound the videotape back to the movie. "It said she played a handmaiden called Wing Wong."

"This is awesome," Holly said, munching popcorn again. "We rock. I want to see what Dickey McBride's Chinese girlfriend looked like."

Chapter 27

I sat in the little side garden of the small house in Westwood
that belonged to my old cooking teacher, Lee Chen. Liling
Chen, I should say. Or should I say Chen Liling, handmaiden to movie queen Catherine Hill in Chen's one and
only American film.

I sipped a cup of tea as we sat together on white-iron
chairs. Lee Chen had professed herself happy to receive a
late-night visitor. She had not been sleeping well, she told
me.

The evening was cool, and we sat under a little electric
patio heater. As we talked, Lee Chen offered to read mah-
jongg tiles and tell me my fortune. They lay out on the patio
table before us, with the twelve tiles divided between East,
West, North, and South, and the one tile in the center. She
had been turning them over one by one and telling me stories about their meanings.

"You see here," she said, turning over Two Circles. "This
is the Chinese character: *Sung*. It is the pine tree and sym-
bolizes the qualities of the tree, that is, firmness and
strength . . ."

As Lee talked I wondered what I was going to do. It
would be kinder to leave everything as it was. It would be
kinder to walk away, leave questions unasked, let things lie.
Lee Chen was not a young woman. What right did I have to
poke around in her past, dredging up long-buried memories?
Was it honorable to disturb a woman I had been so fond of

Chien is a double-edged sword that denotes a balance or a decision . . ."

I knew I had to make a decision. How long could I allow this woman to sit here in friendship, with all the questions I was dreading to ask? I waited for some sign of what I should do with my terrible doubts.

Lee seemed oblivious to my turmoil and continued telling my fortune. "The sword can therefore represent the joining together or the severance of something. For example, in relation to people. Either way it indicates that something is held in balance and that no progress can be made until a decision is made."

"Did you move to America because of a man?" I asked, flat and direct.

Lee Chen looked up. "What do you mean?"

"I find it remarkable that you never mentioned you had been an actress once, long ago."

I watched Lee's eyes and saw in them the look of sudden sadness. "Oh, Madeline. Is this what brings you here to talk this evening? Please, my dear, do not dig and dig at what is better left buried."

"Should we bury the past?"

"Yes," Lee said forcefully. "What is to be served by bringing up such pain? What?"

I looked at Lee, so small, so worried. I hated myself for continuing to hurt her, but would hate myself, too, if I let it all go now.

"You remember the woman named Quita McBride? You met her at Buster Dubin's house."

Lee Chen looked at me and didn't answer.

"She was married to Dickey McBride, the big movie star from long ago. You met her the other night at the Sweet and Sour Club party. And then, later that night, I think you went back to see her. You had something in common with Quita, didn't you? You had both been in love with the same man."

"I do not wish to talk of these things. I know you might mean well, because you are one of the sweetest souls I know. But you must let all this be. It is private business, which has nothing to do with you."

him, I found in myself a sudden boldness. I nodded at him yes, I would.

"That's how we began, my Richard and I. The film company had leased for Richard a beautiful house in Hong Kong, and there I cooked for him and I taught him to play mah-jongg. And soon, I was asked to be in the movie. It was just a very small part. Richard wanted me to be near him, and this was a good way. My parents were very unhappy. But I was eighteen. At that time, the politics in China were very dangerous. My father was busy on the mainland. My cousin was supposed to be watching me closely, but he was too busy gambling."

"And you and Dickey McBride fell in love."

Chen smiled a very sad smile. "I fell in love with him. He told me he, too, was in love. He was an American movie star. He had already been married two times. But he told me I must trust him." Lee's smile vanished. "And I did."

"Did you want to marry him?" I asked.

"With Chinese women, marriage is a very serious thing. In the old traditional values, a wife had four responsibilities. The first is faithfulness: A wife should never consider another marriage even after her husband has died. The second is beauty: A wife should always try to make herself beautiful to attract her husband and make him happy. The third is submissiveness: A wife should understand how to talk with her husband and how to act accordingly and to make him always feel comfortable and never challenged. And last, a wife must be hardworking: She should enjoy cooking, sewing, child rearing and keeping a good, clean and orderly household."

"How terrifying," I said in a small voice, thinking of the millions of women to whom this set of values represented a life of virtual slavery.

"You can see, Madeline, why we traditional Chinese girls were taught to choose a husband with the greatest care. There was no divorce for us. We were bound by honor to only one man, even if he turned out to be a villain. That is different from the modern notions of the West, and even to-

softly, tears again making her eyes shine. "I never should have given away my family's old set. I was a foolish child so many years ago, and I was in love. Richard wanted the tiles, and I had been taught all my life to be submissive, so of course I gave them to him. But what do we know of the passing of time when we are children? I had never imagined that Richard would someday give away my family's heirloom. When I heard that this treasure had been passed to a silly young American girl, I knew I was getting another chance to make amends to my ancestors. That is fate, Madeline. That is why I was meant to be at that party and meet that girl. I went to her right after the party. Just after you drove away to your meeting with your young man, I turned my car around and drove back up to the house. I walked up the steps and heard fighting inside the house. Buster Dubin was fighting with his girlfriend. I kept quiet because I did not want to disturb them. But later, she came outside. I knew it was my chance. I told the girl I wanted to buy the mah-jongg set."

This was my worst fear. Lee Chen had just admitted to being on the stairs with Quita on the night Quita fell to her death. I could imagine a hatred growing in Lee Chen's heart. She had been poorly treated by Dickey McBride, years ago, used and abandoned. She had borne him a child that he ignored. In her pride, she had chosen to take no money from McBride, but how well did that proud decision sit all those long years? As a single mother in a foreign country, how had she managed when her child needed medicine and schoolbooks and clothes? How had Chen felt as years went by and she read about McBride, who continued taking lovers and wives, living a rich man's life?

Is that how her years went? If so, what a bitter time that must have been. And if Chen Liling had kept all this secret pain hidden away for decades, what action would she take when fate brought her to the Sweet and Sour Club party on Chinese New Year? How dizzying was the blow of meeting up with her past ghosts so unexpectedly? The brutal coincidence of running into Dickey's pretty young wife. His blond wife. That certainly might have unhinged quiet Lee Chen.

These thoughts made my stomach twist as I looked at her.

family's mah-jongg set as she had promised. She said I must give her the money first. I told her no and left."

"When you returned," I said quietly. "It was three o'clock, wasn't it? You argued."

"No, no," Lee said. "We said unpleasant words because she did not have my property, that is all."

"Do you have your purse here, Lee?" I asked. I had gone too far not to be absolutely sure I was right. But if I was right, what had I chosen to do?

"What? My purse?" Lee was startled at the turn in the conversation.

"Yes. Could you lend me twenty dollars?"

"Twenty dollars? Of course I will. But what is this about?"

I sat there, waiting for her to fumble with the clasp on her small black-leather bag. She pulled out a wallet and unrolled a tidy stack of bills, all twenties. All, I noticed, with little frowny cartoon faces written in blue pen on the corner.

Ray had drawn that graffiti on those twenties. I had bugged him about it and made a big deal out of defacing the money he'd picked up for the party payroll. But those twenties didn't pay for party supplies. Eight of those twenties I had lent to Quita McBride as she watched her world come crumbling down. Quita's lover was deserting her, her boyfriend was kicking her out of his home, her husband had never really been her husband at all, and his estate was as good as gone.

I looked at the twenty-dollar bill Lee laid neatly down on the table on top of my mah-jongg fortune hand. The stupid face glared from the corner of the bill.

In my life, I have always tried to avoid causing anyone any pain. In fact, I am moved always to protect those for whom I care from any and every pain, if I can. I am actually overwhelmed at times by my fear that some sly pain might seep through my hypervigilant protection and cause damage before I can stop it or soothe it away. I feel panicked at the responsibility of it.

I realized, here, sitting in Lee Chen's rose garden at night, that I probably would never choose to have children of my

"And? If that is true—what then?" she asked, her eyes openly hostile. Her voice a harsh challenge.

"Then, I think Quita must have been very angry with you, Lee. When you came back to see her, it was three o'clock. Quita did not have the mah-jongg case. She had used it as bait to trick you to bring her the money she demanded."

"She was a lying whore," Lee said. "I spit at her. I told her who I was, that I was Richard's wife. She called me all kinds of horrible things, hurtful things. She threw money at me and said, 'go away, old woman, and let me be.' She promised if I withdrew my claim, she would be generous with me. She would send me more twenties."

"And you pushed her. You wanted her to die," I said.

"She was a very bad lady," Lee said, as if she was tired of explaining to a child why she had been forced to step on a beetle. "She made her own terrible life."

"And you ended it," I said aghast, finally believing it to be true. "Why?" I shouted.

"I have been ill, Madeline. I don't talk about it to my daughter."

"You're sick?"

"And who will fight the whore to get Richard's money for his daughter, my Yang, and her daughters, too? Who will make the lawyers give the money? No one. I have never told a soul about Richard. Not even his daughter knows who her real father was. And there was that whore, standing on the stairway, telling me she would never stop fighting to get Richard's money, even if it meant keeping the case open in the courts for years and years and all the money in Richard's accounts were drained dry with the cost of lawyers and fees." Lee was breathing hard. "And that whore said she would tell my daughter that Richard had been her father. I yelled at her to stop, but she wouldn't. She kept telling me the most vile rubbish, and I could not let her do those terrible things she said."

"So you pushed her?" I demanded.

"Yes," Lee yelled.

"You wanted Quita to die?"

Chapter 28

Sunday morning in Los Angeles. One of the places I like to start Sundays is the ABC Seafood Restaurant on the corner of Ord and New Hope in Chinatown. The noise and bustle of its Dim Sum rooms, the lively flavors of a dozen varieties of steamed dumplings, the sounds of Chinese languages, the faces of the hundreds of Chinese-born customers, transport me to a land where life is much different from the one I'm sentenced to live out here in LA. It's Hong Kong, freeway close.

I needed a cheap, quick escape from a night that brought no comfort or rest. I couldn't stay home with my thoughts. Dull from exhaustion, I sought the comfort of routine. Sunday mornings at ABC.

This Sunday morning was more dramatic than most in Chinatown. In order to welcome the Year of the Snake, many of the large Dim Sum palaces, like ABC, had made contributions to neighborhood organizations. These groups brought their musicians and their lion dancers. I stood out on the sidewalk, waiting for Honnett to show up, watching the New Year celebration swirl around me.

Half an hour ago, the lady inside the large restaurant had taken my name and handed me a paper number. Meanwhile, the waiting crowds were gathering outside the front door of ABC Seafood. Not far away, the gunshot ricochet of firecrackers snapped. Firecrackers, I knew, chased away the mythical monster, Nian, which once terrorized the people.

tionship over the years, he'd never blown a job. No one quits a pilot in mid-production. People get fired, but no one walks away. "What happened?"

"I figured you are always right, so I must be wrong." He smiled. "I was too obsessed with the sitcom, with the whole business. So I walked off."

The end of his speech was slightly obscured by a particularly loud drumbeat as the Chinese drummers moved closer to where we stood.

"So what do you want, Arlo?"

"I don't know," he said, looking at his boots, smiling a little. "Maybe I want a hug good-bye."

I leaned forward, wondering if I'd heard correctly. He held me for a moment and let go.

"Yep. Simple as that. I want to be your friend."

"Are you asking for another chance? Because—"

"No, no, no. I get it. We're not going to do that again. I just always thought you'd be in my life, somehow." His eyes crinkled in the corners as he stood there on the street curb in Chinatown, smiling at me, as the lion dancers swooped in the background.

"We can try it," I said, not knowing what else to say. "If you'd like. What are you going to do without your pilot?"

"That's another thing I wanted to talk to you about, actually," he said.

The outside loudspeaker emitted a blare: "Ninety-three."

I looked at the scrap of paper in my hand. Ninety-three.

"That's my number," I said.

Arlo put his hand on the back of my leather jacket and guided me through the crowd watching the dancers. He opened the door of the restaurant and walked me in.

It was noisy and crowded inside the door. The hostess was talking into a microphone mounted on a podium. "Ninety-three?" she said. "Ninety-four?"

"Ninety-three," I said loudly, catching her eye.

She gave us a small, professional smile, and beckoned Arlo and me to follow.

Inside the entry, dozens of customers waited for tables. Almost every face looked to be Chinese. They squeezed in

Arlo turned to me. "A guy? You're already seeing some-one else? I thought you were meeting Sophie for lunch."

I shook my head, wondering what fresh hell was this.

The thing is, the men knew each other. Arlo had met Hon-nett on a few occasions. Work occasions. But by Arlo's star-tled sick new expression, anyone could see that everything had changed. The idea hit him hard. Honnett and me. This was clearly a whole new world of pain into which Arlo had unerringly plopped himself.

Ignoring Honnett, Arlo turned at me, his eyes reproachful. "You left me for a policeman? How does this possibly fig-ure, Mad? I thought it was the *hamburger bun*—the food thing. I can be picky. I know this. It's like a religious differ-ence between us."

I gave Honnett a quick look, to see how he was doing with this scene. He was clearly not having a picnic, but he wasn't bolting either. I admired his ability to take the stress.

Arlo took my glancing at Honnett as evidence of the deepest sort of betrayal. I was sharing a look with another man. He had more to say. "Madeline . . . a *cop*? A lousy cop?" His voice was getting louder, but he did turn to Hon-nett, and say, "No offense." Then back to me. "So how long have you been dating this guy? Must be months. How long have you been playing around?"

"Wait." I looked at him, hoping to get through before I was truly never able to come to any restaurant I liked again, having had these bad scenes with Arlo haunting me in each and every one. "We're not going to do this. I just can't. I'm a wreck. Nothing was going on behind your back, whether you want to believe me or not. Please. You know we weren't working. And it wasn't about the bun."

Arlo looked crestfallen. "What then?" He thought it over. "*The Empty Pot*? Was that it?"

I felt uncomfortable. But I suppose everyone needs to hear it one more time, spelled out. "Yes, Arlo. It was. Kind of. That little story symbolized what we were up against, you and I. The big gulf between how you think and how I think."

"*The Empty Pot*," Arlo explained to Honnett, including

Honnett continued, "But since you asked me, I do think the story says something else. I think it talks about the nature of emptiness, don't you?"

"Emptiness?" Arlo repeated.

"Right," Honnett said. "It's pretty hard to look inward and acknowledge how empty we are at times, isn't it? Without kids to love. Without a wife to love. Without a job to love. You know what I'm talking about, Arlo? Without God to love. That kind of emptiness is profound. And people tend to hide from it, rather than facing it and fixing their lives if they can."

Arlo was silent. A first. And then he asked, "Are we talking about the same kids' book, because . . ."

"Sure," Honnett interrupted in a calm voice. "Ping's power was not just in admitting he had failed the emperor's test. He had the strength to own his emptiness. He accepted himself, even in failure."

"Oh," I said, and Honnett looked at me. It might have been the most romantic moment of my life, considering the circumstances.

"Well, I gotta be going," Arlo said, scraping his chair back and standing. "This has been great. We ought to do this every Sunday."

"Arlo . . ." I said, wondering what would come of us all, and not up to any more deep thoughts.

"Just kidding," Arlo said. But we're going to stay friends, right? You promised me that."

I looked at him.

"Okay, I'll just wrap it up quickly," Arlo said. "One. We're going to be friends. Two. You think my new movie deal is fine."

Arlo Zar would never change. Or maybe he would. I only knew I wouldn't be there to see it.

Arlo stood by the table for a moment, staring at me. "Well. Bye, Maddie," he said, then he turned and left in a hurry.

"That seemed civilized," Honnett said, smiling at me after Arlo cleared out.

I laughed. I always appreciate sarcasm.

mind. Who else had to know what had really happened on that quiet night in Whitley Heights? I tried to convince myself no one would be hurt, but the truth, painful as a toothache, would not allow such an easy resolution. There were two women to whom I was obligated in this matter. One I had cared for, one I had not, but was either of their lives more or less important? If I chose to protect Lee Chen's secret, how would I live with myself as I betrayed Quita McBride once again?

In the end, the hours spent weighing and judging and agonizing were all a waste. As dawn came and my bedroom window began to brighten, I had come up with no plan that would make everything all right. I drifted off to sleep.

When I awoke an hour later, I recognized my own truth. I was powerless to right a situation that was so wrong. Lee Chen had admitted to pushing a woman to her death. Fated or not to the lives we live in this world, I still believe we must make our own choices. It was as simple as that. This was true for Lee Chen, and also for me.

Calling Honnett was like calling the doctor when you have spent the night denying you felt a lump—that kind of anguish. There was little relief in coming forward with such devastating news.

During that phone call, Honnett remained quiet as I told him everything that I had learned, everything that Lee Chen had revealed to me the night before. We agreed to meet at eleven. I selected the location.

A succession of servers pushing steaming carts stopped at our table and left off a selection of treats. And now the table before us was covered in little metal bowls filled with four tiny Dim Sum treats each, from spicy pork Shu Mei to succulent pink shrimp Har Gow to Ho Yip Fan, fried rice wrapped in lotus leaves. There were also soup dumplings, a marvel of culinary engineering in which a portion of soup is magically sealed inside a gossamer rice-flour skin and steamed without a drop of leakage, and Chien Chang Go, "thousand-layer cake with egg topping," each small pastry tart a piece of flaky sweetness.

have said it in the past. "Say," I said, "I got a call from Catherine Hill. How about that?"

"Movie stars are calling you. That's perfect," Honnett said, grinning.

"The maj 'girls' wanted to invite me to their next mah-jongg party. Next Friday."

"Really?" Honnett looked up, a dumpling poised between chopsticks, and asked, innocently, "To play or to cook?"

I had to smile at that. "To play. They want to teach me. I think I remind them of themselves as young women. Which is pretty scary, Honnett."

"You can teach them a thing or two," he said.

"Oh, and Wesley has a weird thing," I said. "You know that house he's been fixing up. He's already replaced the roof, floors, plaster, almost everything. And then guess what? He got a call from a broker who has a buyer with cash. They are making an offer."

"I thought you told me the house isn't finished," Honnett said.

"Right. But most of the major work is done. Wesley has poured a ton of money into it already. But here's the catch. The new buyer wants to tear the entire house down and start over. They're going to put up a new one from scratch."

"Ouch," Honnett said, getting the irony. "Are they offering a lot?"

"Oh, yeah," I said. "Wes will make a fortune. But he'll lose the Wetherbee house."

"Tough call," Honnett said. "Someone wants to destroy all his work."

I smiled at Honnett, feeling better than I had in days. This felt like a relationship. This felt good.

"Will he sell it?" Honnett asked, sampling the pork Shu Mei.

"Oh, yeah," I said, smiling. "It's a lot of money. He is really aggravated and worried about it, but he can't stop the world from changing."

"I had no idea Wes had such a tough business head," Hon-